The Bossman's Daughters 3

Aryanna

Lock Down Publications and Ca$h Presents
The Bossman's Daughters 3
A Novel by *Aryanna*

Aryanna
Lock Down Publications
P.O. Box 870494
Mesquite, Tx 75187

Lock Down Publications
Like our page on Facebook: Lock Down Publications @
www.facebook.com/lockdownpublications.ldp
Cover design and layout by: **Dynasty Cover Me**
Book interior design by: **Shawn Walker**
Edited by: **Lashonda Johnson**

Stay Connected with Us!

Text **LOCKDOWN** to 22828 to stay up-to-date with new releases, sneak peaks, contests and more...

Thank you!

Submission Guideline.

Submit the first three chapters of your completed manuscript to ldpsubmissions@gmail.com, subject line: Your book's title. The manuscript must be in a .doc file and sent as an attachment. Document should be in Times New Roman, double spaced and in size 12 font. Also, provide your synopsis and full contact information. If sending multiple submissions, they must each be in a separate email.

Have a story but no way to send it electronically? You can still submit to LDP/Ca$h Presents. Send in the first three chapters, written or typed, of your completed manuscript to:

LDP: Submissions Dept
Po Box 870494
Mesquite, Tx 75187

DO NOT send original manuscript. Must be a duplicate.

Provide your synopsis and a cover letter containing your full contact information.

Thanks for considering LDP and Ca$h Presents.

Dedication

This book is dedicated Connor and Natalie. I love you both and I'll see you soon.

Acknowledgements

I thank God first for the blessings and the struggle. It gets real. I would like to thank my significant other, who I love very much. I don't have the words to sum up everything you mean to me but I pray that you know anyway. I have to thank my family for just being who you are and being stubborn enough not to change. I love you. I have to thank my fans and supporters for ev-er-y-thing! I'm still doing it for you all. I especially have to thank my LDP riders for supporting me through the good the bad and the ugly. And to Cash, egos aside, we do this shit. Before I forget I have to thank those who hate me and hate on me. I know you can't see me right now but I'm sticking my tongue out bitch! Lol! And now for the roll call let me shout out all the people I like first Llewellyn(You're an asshole), but you're from Pittsburg so it's ok. ;Maurice Hegman (global/ Hoover-Texas standup) ;Slim Brim ;Bowman (Roidrage) ;Yates (You're a asshole and your white but it's been a privilege) ; buddy Davis (thanks for the job sorry it didn't work out) ;Sherrie (NASCAR needs a driver like you). Special shout out to Kristen Jones my favorite nurse I apologize for exposing your affair unintentionally, next time don't tell lies on people. And to Luke Houston I know what you did last summer. If I forgot anyone else good or bad, don't worry there's another book coming out soon.

Aryanna

Chapter 1
Freedom

My experiences in life have taught me that pain comes in two forms, physical and emotional. Both can destroy you depending on the situation you find yourself in, but it's not guaranteed. I guess that's why they say what doesn't kill you makes you stronger. Bet the mufucka who thought of that slogan didn't experience both types of pain at once, and if he or she did they were contemplating suicide. I know that just as surely as I knew this lil' nigga was trying to rip me in half, and I was wishing for a gun, as bad as I was for some more of that good dope they started this process with.

"Come on, Free, push baby, you're almost there."

"Mufucka, I am p-pushing! Shut up." I growled, glaring at Bone, squeezing his hand tighter as another contraction rocked me.

All the shit I've seen in movies is true, although I always believed it was exaggerated for dramatic effect. I really did wanna kill this nigga one minute and tell him how much I loved him the next. All in the same breath, I was swearing off dick forever. It had led to the second most painful experience in my life.

The most painful had been losing my father. Even though, I understood that was a pain that would never go away. I felt like I was underwater drowning, because I was thinking about him while my son forced his way into the world. Emotionally and physically the pain in this room right now was next level, but there was no escape.

"Okay, Freedom, the baby is crowning so I want you to push," Dr. Liam said, scooting further between my legs.

She didn't have to tell me this little nigga was crowning. I'd felt every single move he made since he decided today was a good day to move out of me. At first, I wasn't mad because carrying him for nine months had given me aches and experiences, I'd never forget, nor wanted to relive. I hadn't anticipated how much it would hurt though.

"I fucking hate you, you did this to *me!*" I screamed at Bone, wishing for any type of weapon to turn on his ass right now.

The fact that he was smiling down at me, dabbing my forehead with a cool washcloth only pissed me off more. Even though, I knew I'd be homicidal mad if he wasn't here.

"One more push, Free, just one more big push," Dr. Liam coached.

If she was lying, I would kill her for it later. But for now, I gritted my teeth, closed my eyes, and pushed hard enough to rocket my son into my doctors waiting arms. The moment he was out of me I felt a relief unlike anything I'd known, and it only succeeded in adding more tears to the ones already streaming down my face. Bone and Dr. Liam probably thought my tears were ones of joy like most new mothers, but they weren't.

This whole experience hadn't been surreal like I heard it would be, because the cloud of my father not being here for this moment was a very real thing. How could I know joy even in this moment? I couldn't stop seeing my daddy's face whether my eyes were open or closed, knowing he died because of me?

Because of my son, I had chosen to do what everyone had considered to be the right thing. The motherly thing, and it had cost me the one person I couldn't bear to lose. How could I ever be happy again knowing this?

"He's beautiful, Free, absolutely beautiful," Bone said, crying as he watched the Dr. inspect and clean his namesake.

Very few knew that Bone's real name was Bartholomew Robertson, but he wanted his son to be named after him, so the secret was out. Of course, he insisted we call him B.J. and to anyone who asked that stands for Bone Jr.

I could see the look of love and pride etched in every line of his face. His eyes twinkled with a sparkle, that had never been there before as he looked at his son.

There was no doubting he'd cut the umbilical cord when I wasn't paying attention and probably put it in his pocket as a souvenir. This was easily the best moment of his life. If the smile on his face and love in his eyes was any indication, I couldn't relate.

"You ready to meet your nine pounds, three ounces, son mama?" Dr. Liam asked, passing the baby to Bone, who in turn slowly handed him to me.

He was so tiny I thought I would hurt him and despite the turmoil I felt that wasn't what I wanted at all. He was high yellow in complexion, which would've had most niggas asking for a DNA test given how chocolate Bone was, but I could definitely see my man in my little boy. I could also see his grandfather and this recognition hurt my heart even more than giving birth had. My dad should be here, he should be right here with me, and his grandson, but he wasn't and he never would be.

"Take him," I said, holding him out to Bone.

"But, Free, you didn't even -."

"Just take him!" I said again, slightly raising my voice.

B.J. had been quiet 'til I got loud, now he was adding his high notes to the chorus, but that was okay because it made Bone move faster.

"It's okay, give him to me, I'll take him down to the nursery." The nurse said, coming up next to Bone.

I could tell in his body language by how rigid he was, that he was reluctant to hand B.J. over, but his eyes were on me. I could see worry sliding into where joy had been. It wasn't my intention to ruin this moment for him, I was just feeling overwhelmed.

"Everything looks good, Free, you passed the placenta, and little man didn't rip you open, so there is nothing else

I need to do down here. Just let me clean up and I'll be out of your way," Dr. Liam said.

I didn't verbally respond because I was scared I would tell her not to go. Once her and the nurses were out of the room, there was nothing standing in the way of what was guaranteed to be an awkward conversation. Bone, pulled a chair up beside my bed and sat down, but thankfully he didn't reach for my hand like he normally would have. It wasn't like the thought of his touch was repulsive, I just needed my space. Somehow, I was gonna have to translate that into words that didn't hit him like a bullet between the eyes. It was a long ten minutes before the nurses and Dr. Liam filed out, but once they were gone the room filled with a deafening silence.

"What's wrong, Free?"

"I'm fine it's just been a long day," I replied, looking down at my hands.

"It's been an amazing day, but somehow I don't think that's the description running through your mind right now."

"Don't do this," I said tiredly.

"Do what? Care about you? About whatever is wrong with you? I love you Free which means I care. I know losing your dad hurt, but that was six months."

"Don't minimize my loss by acting like six months is enough time to fucking grieve. Don't pretend to know how I'm feeling, and *don't* fucking judge me," I said forcefully, feeling my anger swim into the deep waters of my depression and made myself at home.

"Baby, that's not what I'm trying to do, I'm trying to understand and help in any way you will let me. I don't know how your feeling, and no matter how much I ask or how many ways I ask, you still don't tell me. I get that you want to be alone to grieve which is why you have avoided your sisters, but I ain't them and I'm not going anywhere."

"Don't I know it," I replied under my breath.

"Excuse me? What the fuck is that supposed to mean, you want me out of your life all of a sudden?"

The bitch in me was tempted to leave this question up in the air just long enough to fuck with this niggas head, but he didn't deserve that.

"What I'm saying is everybody deals with grief differently. Angel and Destiny are halfway around the world and I have no idea how they're dealing with my dad's death. All I know is that it's been hard for me to deal with it with you hovering over me the entire pregnancy. I know you mean well, but baby I can't breathe sometimes."

I'd spoken those words in a normal tone, but the expression on his face looked like I'd screamed at him, and said I wished he was dead. While it's true that I'm a woman, I have yet to master the arts of being gentle or subtle. I spoke my mind, and sometimes that was too much for anyone to handle.

"I-I don't know what you want me to say," he stammered, clearly caught off guard by what I had to say.

"There's nothing I expect you to say Bone. All I'm asking is for your understanding and a little space."

"And what about B.J.? Do you need space from him, too?" He asked in a somewhat accusing tone.

It was on the tip of my tongue to say some real shit because I felt like he was being overly sensitive, but the more I thought about it the more his question made sense. The ugly truth was that I hadn't even been able to hold the new life I'd brought into this world, because deep down a part of me felt like I'd traded his life for my fathers. From the moment I let him send me and my sisters out of the country, I'd chosen my unborn child over the man who would've laid down his life for me. How did I look at my son and not think about that? How could I be the mother he needed when I couldn't look at him, and see the beauty of life, but instead the darkness of death? I didn't know how to answer those questions, but I know how to answer Bone's.

"B.J. is my son, our son, and I don't need space from him," I lied again, looking at my hands so he couldn't peek into the windows of my soul.

"Really? So, why couldn't you hold him for more than a minute? I know part of you blames me for what happened to your dad, but that little boy is innocent in all of this shit. He has a clean slate and it's not fair to make him apart of the past."

Logically, everything he said was right and as much as it hurt to admit, there was some truth to me blaming him for what happened to my father. That didn't mean I was right or that the way I felt was justified in any way. My thoughts and feelings weren't on a logical wavelength and I was woman enough to admit that to myself at least. I couldn't tell Bone the truth because he wouldn't understand.

"Bone, I'm just tired and drained emotionally and physically. Twelve hours of labor will take a lot out of anybody, but I'm sure I'll be better for B.J. once I get some rest," I assured him.

Looking up I found him staring at me hard, no doubt contemplating whether I was full of shit or simply crazy. If he would've asked me I couldn't have given a straight answer that would've stayed the same for ten consecutive minutes. If I could sum up everything in one word I would chose *wrong*. Because that's how everything felt. I had an idea about how to make it right though.

"I completely understand you being tired, and you should get some rest. I'm gonna go down and spend some time with B.J., take some pictures to send to everybody."

"You gotta be careful, you know Angel and Destiny are still wanted in a major way," I reminded him.

The only reason I'd given birth to my son on U.S. soil outside of a prison cell is because the Feds couldn't tie me to shit, but Angel had escaped from jail after shooting up a club and Destiny had helped kill four cops in Chicago. They will forever be hunted, but it wouldn't be me, or Bone who led the law to them. I may not have spoken to them in six months, but I still loved them though.

"Don't worry I'll be careful, you just get some sleep," he said, leaning down, kissing me gently on the forehead.

"I'll be back first thing in the morning."

"I'll be here," I replied, smiling weakly.

I laid back and tried to force my mind to shut off, so I'd stop seeing my father dying in my arms and stop hearing him beg me to do one last thing. I'd lost track of how many times I'd relived every second of my dad's last moments, wondering what I could've done differently. The answer was easy I should've never let him go on the mission of killing my mother by himself. Sure, he was *'Father God'*, an indestructible force as described by anyone who knew him, but more than that he was the man I could always count on.

Where the fuck was I when he needed someone to count on? I'd asked myself that question numerous times too, but now that I had my baby my answer was different. I may not have been there before, but I could be there now by doing what he'd asked of me. I could save the brother I never met and slaughter the mother who'd destroyed my world. I could make shit right and become righteous again.

Laying in my bed I allowed my thoughts to organize themselves until the clock over my door struck 1:00 a.m. Thanks to the wonders of modern medicine, giving birth no longer meant I had to stay on my back for days afterwards. Gingerly I got up from the bed, removed my I.V., and slipped back into the now too big maternity sweat pants I'd had on when I came in. Quickly, I stepped into my New Balance sneakers, and then I traded my hospital gown for my gray Black Billionaire hoodie. After peeking out into the hallway to make sure the coast was clear, I made my way as quickly as possible to the stairway. Within minutes, I was outside on the street, and seconds later, I vanished into the night.

Chapter 2
Destiny

"Really Destiny?" Black Sam asked in obvious disgust, as he stood just outside the balcony door.

"What?" I asked startled, but not breaking stride, or slowing down in the gallop I was doing on the nigga beneath me.

It was understood between me and Black Sam, dick would be involved in our relationship, but the expression on her face said now wasn't the time. At least I wasn't fucking him in our bed without her.

"Al-most done," I panted, grabbing the back of the lounge chair we were on for leverage, so I could ride him harder.

Thankfully, she didn't stay to watch, but instead went back into the house. This dick was good and I wanted to enjoy every minute on it. The dude it was attached to spoke very little English, but knew how to please a pussy, and that was all that mattered. The way he reached around and grabbed ahold of my ass turned me on so much, I came for the third time since he'd been inside me. I was mad now that I was gonna have to get up.

"W-why you stop?" He asked, still moving beneath me, sending shock waves through my body.

"My Senorita is mad, Grande mad. We'll finish this later," I said, climbing off of him, searching for my bikini bottoms to put back on.

It wasn't my intention to tease him or give the wrong impression when I bent over to retrieve my swimsuit, but apparently that's what I did. Before I knew it, he was behind me and back inside me. I opened my mouth to object, but he was already pounding me with back shots that had me reaching for the lounge chair, so I wouldn't fall.

"Hurry," I moaned, throwing the pussy back at him.

I don't know what he was mumbling in Spanish, but the way his dick was throbbing with each stroke, and the trembling told me he was almost there. I could already feel my juices running down my leg, but the treatment he was giving me had me moments away from adding to that flood.

"That's right, fu-fuck me Papi!" I demanded, cummin' hard enough to make my knees wobble.

Seconds later, I felt him pull his dick out of me before hot cum shot all over my ass cheeks. In all the excitement, I'd forgotten, I told him to never cum in me, even with a condom on. Brazil had the highest AIDS rate next to Africa, and you couldn't tell who had it because everyone was so damn beautiful. They weren't shy about fucking either. I stayed bent over long enough for Felipe to wipe his cum off of me, then I put my bikini bottoms on.

"Back to work," I told him, kissing my fingers before placing them on his lips.

This may have looked weird to anyone watching considering how intimate we'd just been, but Samantha was the only person I kissed, period.

After picking up my bottle of Grey Goose from the side of the pool, I made my way inside our house to see what had my girl's panties in a twist.

"Okay, I know your mad, but I don't know why," I said, taking a swig from the bottle in my hand, joining her at the kitchen table, overlooking the pool and backyard.

"The pool boy, *really*? How much of a cliché are you, drinking in the middle of the day, and fucking the help?"

"You trippin', that mufucka is *fine* and the dick on point. All three of us need to get down for real, because it's obvious you need some stress relief and-"

"Nah, what I need is that boss bitch, I fell in love with to stop acting like a goddamn lush or Hollywood wife and get back to who we were," she said, with obvious attitude.

Her tone of voice stopped the bottle headed for my lips in mid-air, causing me to look at her closer, and fight off the buzz of alcohol clouding my brain. While it was true we'd been through too much to have secrets, or be anything other than honest with each other, Samantha didn't talk to me like this. Black Sam was beautiful, intelligent, and loyal, but she wasn't no badass, and I'd never seen her get out of her skin, until now.

"Say what?" I asked, slowly.

"You heard what I said. I've known you for years and I've always accepted whatever comes with you, even before we got into a relationship. Why? Because you were Destiny Walker, a bad bitch I couldn't help but respect because of how you moved. I don't see that same woman now, though. This bitch here smokes weed, drinks all day, and fucks random niggas. Then curls up with me at night when the liquor still doesn't numb the pain. I don't know who you are, but it's pathetic," she said, shaking her head slowly.

Her words had me reaching for my pistol, causing me to forget I was in a bikini, therefore unarmed. She was definitely using her words as a weapon, I wanted something to level the playing field.

"What are you reaching for, *this*?" she asked, holding up the little .25 Caliber pistol I normally carried at all times.

Searching my memory, I couldn't remember the last place I'd left it, and based on the conversation we were having I didn't feel very comfortable with it in her hands.

"I was just scratching my back," I lied.

"Now see, the bitch I used to know wouldn't have even come out her face with some lame shit like that, but I guess you really ain't yourself. You wanna shoot me, Destiny? Why, for telling you the truth you need to hear? If Freedom or Angel could see you, they'd kick your mufuckin' ass and you *know* it. You wanna shoot the messenger, though, right? Well, do it, then," she said, sliding the gun across the table.

It skidded to a stop right next to the liquor bottle, almost like it was taunting me, telling me to choose.

"On second thought, you might be better served to put the gun in your mouth and pull the trigger," she said cruelly.

The coldness in her tone was as brand new as her attitude and the way she was talking to me. The only thing that stopped me from picking the gun up, emptying the clip into her beautiful face was the fact that she was telling the truth. Every word spoken and accusation leveled was the truth. She wasn't allowing me to hide from that anymore.

Despite how cold her words were, the tears slowly slid down her face and the love in her hazel eyes told me how much she really cared. How hurt she was by having to watch me lose myself. It wasn't like I wanted to be this way. I didn't feel strong enough to face all the bullshit with my life at the moment. Not only had I lost my father, who I didn't even get to say a proper goodbye to. I'd lost the *only* mother I'd ever known because Free refused to talk to me. I knew she wasn't speaking to Angel either. Bone, told us, it wasn't because she blamed us in any way. *She blamed herself.* I didn't know how to grieve for all we'd lost, but I felt we needed each other to do it properly.

Since that wasn't a possibility, I just did my own thing, my own way. Living life on my terms because no one cared or was affected except me. Or so, I'd thought until this conversation began. Now it was evident that I was hurting Samantha and considering that she'd given up her whole life and pledged allegiance to me in this foreign country, I owed her better than that.

"What do you want me to say?" I asked softly, pushing the gun back across the table to her.

"I don't want you to say shit. I want you to be the woman I fell in love with."

"You're still in love with me?" I asked, smiling despite the tears I felt in my throat.

"Bitch, if I wasn't in love with you, I'd have left a long time ago. I've been with you every step of the way. It was me who came and told you and Angel what happened that night, and that was an incredibly hard thing to do. I knew it would destroy you. I did it anyway because I couldn't let you go through that by yourself. I know our relationship will never be what one would call normal, but I'm yours and you're mine, and I need you to get back to how you use to be."

Despite how hard she'd come for my head moments ago, I couldn't stop smiling. I knew she was kickin' real talk to me. Her and Free had been the only two to stay when the rest of us fled the country, and she always had a special place in my heart for her willingness to stay on the frontline. Even if it was behind a computer. The love and loyalty she was giving wasn't something I could take for granted, but that was exactly what I'd been doing, and it had to stop.

"Thank you. Not just for always being there when I needed you, but for saying the shit I didn't wanna hear," I said, sincerely.

"You don't gotta thank me, but you do gotta be better so-"

"You know you want, come, we share," Felipe said.

I turned to see him standing in the doorway asshole naked, dick on full tilt, ready to do damage.

In his mind, he'd probably thought Black Sam's attitude had been about me fucking him, but it was deeper than that, and sex wasn't gonna fix it. I opened my mouth to tell him this, but I didn't get the chance before his face exploded like a smashed watermelon. Turning back to Black Sam I found her with my pistol still smoking in her hand. To my knowledge she'd never dropped the hammer on an actual person, and to see her do it now showed me how much our roles had switched.

"What the fuck? Why'd you do that?" I asked, confused.

"It was obvious, he didn't know his place, and I aint got time to explain it to him. I chose the easiest solution."

"Who are you?" I asked, shaking my head, looking back at the dead, naked pool boy sprawled on the grass outside the balcony door.

"You know who I am. Right now, the focus needs to be on getting you back to being who you are, because we've got shit to do."

The way she said this brought my attention back to her. She sounded like she did back in the day when there was a situation to handle.

"What's going on?" I asked.

"Get yourself together first, then we'll talk," she replied, standing up, putting the gun back in her pocket before going outside, and dragging the body out of sight.

I left the bottle of Grey Goose on the table, then made my way upstairs into the bathroom. I was hesitant to turn on the light and face my failures in the mirror, but tripping and breaking my neck on the marble floor wouldn't help me either.

I turned the light on, giving my eyes time to adjust, and then I turned the blistering hot shower on before going to my side of the double sink and brushing my teeth. Once that was done I stripped my swimsuit off and stepped into the steam-filled shower with hopes of cleansing more then just my body.

The water was soothing and my body felt relaxed from the sex, but as the alcohol buzz completely faded, and my brain began to clear the tears came. They always did when I was sober, which was why I stayed high or drunk 24/7.

Free wasn't the only one blaming herself for what happened to dad, especially since my part in knocking off some cops was the reason all of us couldn't be there when shit went down. If Lil' Boy and I had chilled maybe shit would've played out differently. I had to live with the decision I'd made, but I didn't know how to do that without being swallowed by guilt. All I knew at this point was that I was gonna have to find a way through because my father didn't raise no bitches or no suckas. Thankfully, we'd surrounded ourselves with good people so none of us had to endure this rough time alone.

For now, being alone was what I needed, I vowed that this would be my last cry of self-pity. I would forever mourn my father, but in the right way. It was a full hour before I was strong enough to come from underneath the waters spray, but it felt like I'd left a ton of bricks behind me. The trick now was not to pick them up again. When I came out of the bathroom, Black Sam was sitting on the bed doing something on her laptop, so I decided to get dressed before round two of our conversation kicked off.

"Where did you put the body?" I called from inside the closet.

"I'ma have him buried beneath the rose bushes, don't worry. Hurry up and get dressed, we gotta go."

"Go, go where?" I asked, pulling on a white T-shirt and some blue jean booty shorts. "Didn't you hear me?" I asked, coming back into the bedroom.

"I heard you. Do you wanna see pictures of your nephew?"

"My n-nephew? Oh my God, Free, had her baby!" I squealed, rushing to sit next to her, so I could see her laptop screen.

The light skin little butterball looking back at me was simply beautiful, he brought tears to my eyes. I could definitely see Free and Bone in his features, but I saw some of my dad too, which I knew had to make Free happy.

"He's so fucking cute. I know Free is glad to have finally dropped his big ass though," I said laughing.

"He is cute, almost makes me want one of my own."

This statement caused me to look at her because kids wasn't something we'd discussed, but I wasn't against it.

"Do you-"

"We can have that conversation later, right now we've got other things to worry about," she said, cutting me off.

"Okay, so what's going on?"

"Do you notice how your sister isn't in any of these pictures with the baby, just Bone?"

I hadn't actually noticed until she brought it up, but now that she had I noticed how weird that was.

"Why is that?" I asked.

"According to Bone, Free held little B.J. for all of thirty seconds before she passed him back to Bone, now she's gone."

"What the fuck do you mean *gone*?" I asked, feeling more than just a touch of panic come over me.

"I mean she left the hospital sometime last night. Bone has no idea where she is, and he's scared because she's not herself. He has no idea where she's going, or what she's gonna do."

I haven't talked to Free in six months, so to hear all this was an absolute shock. Despite, us not talking I still knew what she was up to, it was the only thing that made sense. She was going after Sapphire, and nothing would stand in her way.

Chapter 3
Angel

"Some of the girls wanna talk to you."

"Send them in," I told Lil' Boy, leaning back in my leather chair, rubbing my eyes, to clear the stars away from staring at the computer too long.

A boss's job was never done, but I wasn't complaining, because work was the only thing that kept the depression at bay. In these last six months, my whole world had changed in every way possible. If someone would've given me the option, of either sitting on death row still having my dad alive, and my sisters still being the lungs I needed to breath. Or to be on the run in Russia, running a strip club, without my dad and sisters, the decision would've been a no brainer. I wasn't given that choice though. The cards were dealt and I had to play the hand in front of me or die.

The disturbing part was that as more days passed, death didn't seem like a bad option, or alternative. Some might say, I was on my poor little rich girl shit. I was sitting pretty making money, hand over fist, minus what had to be kicked up to the Kremlin for the Russian government looking the other way, so I shouldn't have any complaints.

They didn't know how much value went into real family, how much loyalty mattered more than riches. Jadakiss, said it best, *'I'd rather be broke together than rich alone.'* The only problem was, that wasn't an option anymore. I couldn't bring my father back to life and the glue that held the family together just wasn't sticking. My mind turned to the business at hand, as seven of my most beautiful dancers were shown into my office, then lined up side-by-side in front of my desk.

This was a united front if I'd ever seen one. "What can I do for you ladies?" I asked.

"I will speak for everyone," A statuesque blonde named, Sasha said in somewhat broken English.

Her tone was not demanding nor aggressive, but it was all business, I could respect that. She was standing in the middle with three girls to the left and right of her.

I turned my attention to her. "Talk to me, Sasha," I said, leaning back in my chair.

"Are you the new boss?" she asked, fidgeting slightly.

"I'm in charge for now, yes."

"You have been in the club running the daily operations for months, so this is your club."

The way she said this, sounded more like a statement than a question. But, I was still unclear about where she was going with this.

"If there's a problem, Sasha, you can talk to me. I'll do my best to fix it."

"No, there's no problems. We like you and you treat us good. Other girls from other clubs want to dance here. But only if they work for you. You used to dance, so you know and you treat us fair. We make more money and keep more too without being downgraded or mistreated. Other women not so lucky. Before you came it was not this way. Are you staying?" she asked.

Finally, even with how thick her accent was, I understood completely what she was saying. As well as what she wasn't saying. The laws in this country were different from the U.S., women definitely weren't equal over here. I only know how to be one way. The treatment I offered these women, was the same I'd gotten when I danced. Big Baby and Lil' Boy, made sure that sentiment was enforced.

I didn't own the club though, Kamile did. The only problem was, no one had seen, or heard from her in over four months. I had to step up and take over, since this was where the three of us were hiding out. The strip club was a business I knew and understood, plus it was a more than welcomed distraction from the chaos that was my life. It was only temporary though. Despite Kamile's fear of Free, she'd made all the arrangements to get me, Lil' Boy, and

Big Baby set up here. But a couple weeks later, no one could find her.

My first thought was that my sister had killed her. Even though Bone, assured me while she was pregnant, he wasn't letting her do a damn thing. Then I thought Kamile, had just gone underground, but that didn't fit. Because even if she had, she would've checked on her businesses. She was too much of a workaholic not to.

I didn't know what happened to her, but I'd kept club *Private Dancer* open and doing smooth business. Even though, I had to kill the mufucka she'd left in charge, because his fingers were sticky, and he couldn't keep his dick out of the girls. Even when they didn't want it. I understood why the ladies wanted me to maintain leadership and control, but I didn't know how long that would last.

"Sasha, I won't lie to any of you. I really don't know how long I'll be here. I do know the owner personally, I can promise shit will never go back to how it was. All of you will be treated like women, not sex slaves, or property, and you're gonna make the money you've been making these last four months." I vowed.

"If you leave you need muscle to keep changes in place. I have a brother who is an ex KGB. I want you meet him for security purposes."

I didn't know a lot about Russia, but I knew their KGB was like our C.I.A, which meant her brother was kind of a big deal. It didn't hurt to know people like that. There was one universal truth that reached every corner of the world, cash ruled everything.

"We'll schedule a meeting. In the meantime, if you have friends who wanna come dance here, bring them to me. I'll meet with them," I said.

Sasha turned to one of the girls and said something in fluent Russian, causing the girl to quickly leave the office. I thought she might've been going to get the potential new girls now, but she returned moments later with a bottle of Vodka and handed it to Sasha.

"You give your word that all will be well, we'll believe you," Sasha said, taking a healthy drink from the bottle, before passing it across the desk to me.

It wasn't even 11:00 a.m., but I knew the gesture meant something, so I accepted the bottle of liquor.

"You have my word," I replied, taking a drink, passing it back.

The bottle was then passed along to each woman who took a swig. Once everyone had a drink they filed back out, as quickly as they'd come in.

"What the fuck just happened?" Lil' Boy asked, with a bewildered expression on his face.

"I guess that would be considered a union meeting in this part of the world."

"Ah, so I guess that makes you the new leader, huh?"

"For better or worse, yeah. I'd still like to know where the fuck Kamile is," I said, reaching into my desk for the Ziploc bag of weed I always kept handy.

In the last six months, I'd taken to blowing a lot of bud, it helped with stress and anxiety. Destiny and Free, used to help with both of those things, but it looked like all that was in the past now.

"You still think Freedom got to her?" He asked.

"Bone, says she didn't, I believe him. He's been on her ass like skin ever since she stormed the hotel with absolute disregard the night our dad was killed."

"What about, Destiny? Maybe she went after Kamile on her own," he suggested.

"I don't think so, but I'll ask just to be sure," I replied, rolling a blunt.

I didn't doubt Destiny could or would kill, Kamila. But her life didn't seem to be about that right now. In all my life, I'd never felt so out of touch with my sisters. We used to be one in the same, bonded by the struggles we'd survived together. Now it was like none of that ever happened. What I would give to turn back the hands of time.

"You okay?" He asked, sitting across from me.

"Yeah, why do you ask?"

"Because you look tired as shit. I may not be sleeping with you, but I know you ain't sleeping, that ain't good."

His concern was touching, it meant even more, because I knew it was genuine. Once upon a time, I considered letting him be my first when it came to sexual activities. But so much had happened, I needed a best friend more than a fuck buddy. He'd been everything I needed, I was grateful for that.

"You worry too much, I'm fine." I replied, putting the finishing touches on my blunt, lighting it.

"I know your fine, easily model material. But on the inside, I know you ain't straight. I'm here for whatever you need."

I wanted to take him up on that offer, except I didn't know what the fuck I needed. I knew what I wanted, but that was a moot point, it would never happen. A shrink would probably say, I needed to grieve over my father, that might even be true, but I didn't know how to do that either. All I knew how to do was keep putting one foot in front of the other, until I couldn't anymore.

"I know you're here for me, I love you for that."

"Finally, I'm getting somewhere." He laughed and winked at me.

"Oh, whatever nigga, you know you ain't ready for-"

Our conversation was interrupted by Big Baby, coming through the door, his phone in hand, and a look on his face that was a mixture of happiness and worry.

"What is it?" Lil' Boy asked, taking the phone, his brother was pushing at him.

I watched behind a cloud of smoke as Lil' Boy, studied the screen silently, slowly scrolling through whatever message was on it, before his eyes came up to meet mine.

"Good news, bad news, good news," he said, cryptically.

"Spit it out," I replied, hitting the blunt again bracing myself.

"Free, had the baby, then disappeared. Now Black Sam and Destiny, are on their way here."

My first thought, was he didn't bullshit about ripping the band-aid off, then fear set in.

"What do you mean, Free, disappeared?" I asked slowly.

In response to my question, he passed the phone to me in exchange for the blunt. I took my time reading the message Destiny, sent Big Baby. I tried not to be hurt, since I wasn't hearing this shit directly from her, while absorbing the information. After re-reading it, I reached the same conclusion Destiny did Free, was going after our mother.

Given everything that happened, I didn't want Free out there operating on her own, given the fact Destiny and Black Sam, were headed this way they must've felt the same.

"Where's my nephew?"

"I'm assuming he's in Atlanta with Bone. Your sister ain't say nothing about it. You know Bone, ain't gonna take him on the road looking for Free," Lil' Boy replied, hitting the blunt, passing it to Big Baby.

Sometimes I wished that nigga, Big Baby could talk. However, I knew, no matter what he was here for all of us, whenever for whatever. Despite how far apart we all were and the obvious dysfunction in our family, we were still family and when it came down to it we would close ranks to have each other's back.

"I think Destiny is right, Free, has to be going after Sapphire. I doubt she knows where she is and since she doesn't have Black Sam with her, she's gonna need some way to get the info she's after," I said, contemplating her first move.

"Do you think she's going back to Chicago to see what she can find out there?" Lil' Boy asked, taking the blunt back from his brother, passing it to me.

"I don't know, I mean she's the only one of us that ain't wanted and on the run, but she's too smart to let the feds know she's coming.

They already postponed the trial, Sapphire was supposed to testify in after she killed my dad, because they knew the whole situation was compromised. I doubt they left any bread crumbs for Free, to follow. Then again, it would be the last place the feds would expect Free, to go considering they detained her out there for a week after our dad died.

"You know her better than any of us, even better than Bone, so if you were her where would you stay?" Lil' Boy asked.

I took a long pull on the blunt, while considering the question. I did know my sister, but at the same time, that bitch was a different type of predator. There was nobody she wouldn't go after, she felt like anybody could get it. On the heels of this thought, came a revelation that was so damn crazy it had to be Free's ultimate play.

"Oh God, I know what she's gonna do," I whispered, becoming more frightened the deeper the idea took hold.

"What?" Lil' Boy asked.

"When you're huntin' reptiles, like the ones that live in the swamp called government, you don't start with the tail. You go for the kill, which means going for the head. The director of the F.B.I."

Aryanna

Chapter 4
King Deuce

It was crazy how much the streets changed in as little as five and a half months, but as I crashed into Nashville, I could feel the difference in the air. During my time in the county, I kept my ear to the street. I knew the power vacuum Monster's death had created, but seeing it was a totally different thing. The hoods I drove by looked like war zones, with all the chunks missing out of apartment buildings from .50 Cal and automatic weapon fire. It was evident that only the elite could survive in this jungle, but little did everyone know, there was a new ruler coming to lay claim to the crown. *King Deuce was back.*

Part of me, thought I'd never see the streets again, because I definitely wouldn't snitch. But once again, an angel had saved my life. I'd spent the last five months thinking about her and her sisters, mainly about her though. Her beauty was one thing, but the cloth she was cut from, and the way she carried herself made her the most gorgeous woman I'd ever known. Each day that passed, my mind expanded with the desire to know her in every way.

It had taken awhile, but I'd finally admitted the King, had found his queen and it was time to settle down for good. I couldn't just go to Angel and tell her that though, she probably wouldn't take me seriously given my womanizing past. I had to show her with actions, my first action was to build an empire we could rule over.

It seemed poetic, our story unfolds like that, since it was her trigger play that had beheaded the last king. Literally, I'd been home two weeks and had managed to organize my soldiers. In preparation for what it would take to take over everything Monster left behind. I didn't just wanna control Nashville and Memphis for 5 Deuce Hoover Crips. I wanted the Empire State of town under my leadership. A move like that took more than muscle though. It took money, because money becomes power. My sole purpose for being in Nashville at the moment, was to have a sit down with my connect to re-establish order. I needed to flood the streets with that good dope a.s.a.p. From West to East, everybody knew that if you wanted that come back product you had to go see Jefe.

Some in the streets called him J. Frizzle, to the people he did legit business with he was Jeff, but to me he was Jefe, *The Boss*. I knew a sit down with him would be mandatory to get shit back to the way it used to be. There would be a lot of questions about me being out so soon. It wasn't disrespectful or an insult to my character, because niggas knew who I was and how I got down. But an explanation was required when you came back from the dead. Twenty-five counts of murder, would've had anyone on death row, especially in Tennessee. So, seeing me moving around was like watching one of those paranormal movies. Ten minutes after entering Nashville city limits, I was guiding my 2015 Range Rover Sport SUV to a stop in front of millionaire status, which was Jefe's exotic car lot and detailing service.

Most niggas in this position, would have inspired hate and jealousy, but he kept it so real. You would rather be like him, than knock him off and take his spot. As I stepped from my truck, I noticed the young nigga Rocky, washing a navy-blue Ferrari 430 spider. I knew I'd get a good laugh real quick. Rocky, wasn't a little bit off like some niggas who grew up in the streets tended to be, he was a lot off. He lived in a dream world, where he was a millionaire, making moves like Scarface. Instead of a dude who did an honest day's work for his money.

"What up, lil' bruh?" I asked, walking towards him.

"Shit, you know me, just shinning this bad mufucka up, so me and Yo Gotti can hit the town tonight. You know that's my cousin, right?"

"Oh yeah, I thought Kevin Gates was you cousin?" I asked, trying to keep from smiling at today's lie.

"Nah, Kevin, just my nigga. He be coming to the studio I got to make them hit records. Me, him, Gotti and some bad bitches gonna take Gotti's plane and shoot out to Vegas right quick, so I can pick up my tiger."

"Your what? Nigga did you just say you got a tiger?" I asked, laughing.

"Real talk bruh, I can show you pictures and everything," he replied, dropping the wet sponge he held, reaching into his back pocket.

"Later for all that, bruh, I got a meeting to get to."

"Cool, I'll holla at you later. But keep your ears open for my mixtape 'Millionaire Mobster'," he said, picking up the sponge, going back to washing the car.

It was on the tip of my tongue, to ask if the mixtape was ever coming out, he'd been talking about it for years. Instead, I kept my mouth shut and proceeded into the building. He either needed to become an author or start taking his meds, so reality could set in. Or, become a comedian, with an imagination like his. Whatever he needed was his problem. My problem was behind the door, I now stood in front of. I didn't raise my hand to knock, I knew I'd been on camera since I pulled up. We were in the back of the main building, but Jefe was too smart to box himself in or not see what was coming.

Suddenly, the deadbolt turned, and I came face to face with Jefe's trigger man. Lil' Hustle, who only stood about five-seven on a good day, weighing two-hundred and fifteen pounds, but wasn't to be confused with the light skinned pretty boy type like me. One look in his eyes, you knew he was with all the bullshit most niggas didn't wanna get involved with. But if he fucked with you, you had no worries.

"What's good, bruh?" I asked giving him a pound, as he slowly stepped aside, allowing me to enter.

"Ain't shit, good to see you out. A little surprised though," He said, closing the door behind me, turning the lock.

When Jefe had agreed to meet, I thought it would just be us because he didn't like a lot of people in his business. I was surprised to see not only Hustle, but Mello, and Freaky Zeeky, as well. Both were from Knoxville, and close to Jefe, but for different reasons. Mello was like Jefe's best friend, they got money in a major way together. Whereas Freaky, was a jack of all trades, who would pick up a gun, or brick of dope with equal quickness. All together we were some heavy hitters from all over town, so it was my hope this was a meeting to unify our talents.

"It's good to see you, Jefe, I-"

I was silenced by the raising of his index finger, as he gave his full attention to the glass chess board, sitting atop of the large maple desk between him and Freaky. Mello, was sitting on the loveseat up against the wall to my left and I could still feel Hustle lingering behind me. I wasn't scared though, because there was no beef here. No doubt they all knew and respected Monster, but me taking him out, earned me a new level of respect, too. I waited patiently, watching as Jefe moved a piece that made Freaky sit all the way back in the leather chair, shaking his head.

"Don't be discouraged, you're getting better. But the student, still ain't ready to beat the master," Jefe said, smiling slightly before shifting his eyes in my direction.

"I'm listening," he said, sitting back in his leather swivel chair.

"You already know me, and my home girl put the play down to eliminate Monster, since he came after me. It went down, but shit got sideways when two of his niggas tried to end me, when I stopped to get something to eat. That got me and my girl jammed up. Her people broke her out of jail though, which allowed my lawyer to argue the lack of evidence they had to convict me. Of course, they tried to offer a deal, but all I had to do was ride it out, and let my lawyer earn all that money I paid her ass."

"And so, they let you out, just like that?" He asked skeptically.

"Hell yeah, my nigga, you know murder is the easiest charge to beat. Plus, the one at the restaurant was clear cut self-defense. The gun I used was clean and registered," I replied.

Jefe was the soft spoken type. His stocky build and direct eye contact alluded to intimidation. But he was more so, about calculation, then action. There was no room for threats, threats were nothing more than unnecessary warnings. The silence in the room stretched on for a full two minutes, as he calmly evaluated me, with the same ruthless intensity he applied to chess. Aside from Mello rolling a blunt, no one else moved, or spoke.

"I'm gonna verify all of this, but in the meantime, tell me why you're here," Jefe said.

"I'm ready to get back to the money, my nigga. You know what it is with me," I replied with enthusiasm.

"I don't know about that. It seems like you're in the middle of a war right now. That's not good for my kind of business. Bodies dropping, means more cops come out, you feel me."

"It ain't no war Jefe, if you kill the head, the body will fall. When it comes to Monster and everything he controlled, shit, it's all over except the crying. I got my niggas ready to take over the whole state," I informed him.

"And how you think that's gonna happen, cuz? We just supposed to roll over, and let that happen?" Hustle asked from behind me.

"Come on cuz, you know it ain't even like that, it's all love. The only beef I had was with Monster and that shit is done now. There's plenty for all the homies to eat off, but I'm big homie on 5 Deuce Hoover across the state. I have to solidify my spot, the only way to do that, is making sure my team eats."

"What about the rest of Monster's loyal followers?" Jefe asked.

"I'm on my Beanie Siegel shit, they either gonna get down, or fucking lay down," I replied sincerely.

"You know I fucks with you kid, but I'ma need some type of assurances that you ain't about to fuck up my money or my product."

"Come on bruh, you know that ain't how I move. I had business with the respect it deserves, because everything else is secondary to getting that money. I'm not even asking you to put no work in my hands today. I wanna finish my clean up out here in Nashville. As soon as that's done, I'll be ready to do what I do."

Again, Jefe, sat stone still analyzing my words and from the look of concerted concentration on his face, he was doubting heavily on whether, or not to take the risk. Our business had never been shaky before, but I understood how things changed every day.

"How much you need?" Mello asked, lighting his blunt.

"Uh, about fifty keys to start, but it'll definitely go up, depending on how fast my niggas can spread out and conquer," I replied, slightly confused about why Mello, was asking this question.

He may have gotten money with Jefe, but that didn't make him the boss, so his interjection at this point in the conversation was unusual.

"You got the money for all that, my nigga?" Mello asked, through a cloud of smoke.

"Come on bruh, I wouldn't be here if I didn't. Besides, it takes millions to see billions, that's what I'm focused on."

"I'm gonna tell you like this though, if any unwanted attention, or heat comes our way. If the work somehow gets tricked off or the money don't come out right, that's your ass. Feel me?" Mello asked, still watching me closely.

"Yeah, I'm gonna fuck with him, and see how everything turns out. I got it."

"That's what it is then. I want you to be mindful of how you conduct yourself in Nashville K.D., I've got eyes and ears everywhere. Clean your situation up without drawing more heat," Jefe ordered.

"I got this, bruh," I replied reassuringly.

"I hope so, because I like you, I'd hate for anything to fuck that up."

I opened my mouth to respond, but the sound of a gun being chambered behind me froze the words in my throat. Talk was cheap and the price of fucking up Jefe's business was the highest.

Aryanna

Chapter 5
Freedom

Three Days Later

The open road in front of me, was waving like a mirage, I had no doubt severe lack of sleep was causing this. I'd literally been on the move since walking out of the hospital. Only stopping long enough to go to my house and get my emergency bag in order to disappear. In the line of work known as the hustle, you always had to have an escape route, for months, I'd been planning to use mine after my son was born. Part of me felt bad for leaving him the way I did, but I knew his father would love him enough for the both of us, right now. So, I ran, it wasn't because I didn't wanna be a mother to my child. It was because I couldn't be his mother, until I'd resolved everything involving my dad, I owed him that.

Of course, I knew the feds were most likely still watching me, because my sisters were still at the top of their fugitive list. But not even that, would stop what I had to do. After I'd gotten what I needed from my house. I got straight on the highway to Texas, reaching out to some of my dad's homies, so they could plug me in with their cartel connections. From that point, disappearing was as easy as watching the sun go down.

It was hard traveling, but I was led through the underground tunnels into Mexico, where I spent the night. Then was led through different tunnels, bringing me into Arizona. The risk was huge considering how hard it was to sneak into the U.S., since Trump became president, but money could move any mountain. For a million in cash, I'd gotten safe passage and the all black 2016 BMW 7 series. I was now driving across country to my destination. I had no illusions about how tough the task at hand was and that

I'd need help, but I needed this time alone to organize my thoughts and plan.

The first thing I needed to do though was find somewhere to sleep before I ended up in a ditch. The sign I'd just passed said there was a Best Western motel a mile ahead. It looked like New Mexico was my stop for tonight. After pulling into the parking lot, I made sure to make two complete turns around the building, looking for anything that made me uneasy. The odds were good that only a handful of people knew I was on the move, but none of them, knew where I was.

Undoubtedly Bone's first calls would've been to my sisters, figuring I'd reach out to them, despite my unwillingness to do that recently. I'd lost track of how many times that idea had appealed to me. But I couldn't do it, I didn't know how to face them, seeing those looks of shame, disappointment, or accusation. At least, not until I made shit right for us. I paid for my single bedroom in cash, thankful the night clerk was a woman, so I could avoid unwanted attention.

After driving around, the motel once more to assure my paranoia. I parked, grabbed the backpack from the trunk, and panicky made my way up to room 202. I locked the door, closed the blinds, and with my pistol grip AK-47 in hand. I finally took a deep breath and sank onto the lumpy mattress. I'd expected to feel calm come over me. Now that I was back on the streets with murder as my only companion, but that's not how I felt. My feelings were beyond explanation. But it felt like something was pulling me back to Atlanta. Maybe it was the man I'd left behind, it was more than a little weird to go without him beside me, or maybe it was my son tickling my conscience, calling to me to be the mother I never had.

Laying there in the dead of night, was the time most mustered up the courage to face these hard questions, but if I wanted to survive. I had to leave these questions and emotions hidden. The time had come to inflict pain, instead of simply feeling it without reprieve. I pushed thoughts of the men in my life aside, I sat up, and turned on the bedside lamp, needing to refocus on the man I'd lost. I emptied the backpack on the bed, revealing two extra clips for the AK, a Glock .29 with an extra clip, 50k in cash, paperwork to match my new identity as Kayla Morris, and a listing of all my dad's contacts.

'Father God' was an important man and for that reason his little black book was filled with legends who knew how to return a favor. I wasn't sure what exact favors people owed, but his book listed them in three categories of importance, *Political, Financial, & Emergency.* Despite years in prison, my dad still commanded the respect reserved for rulers of men, so the number of favors owed didn't surprise me. The hard part was knowing who I needed to contact now, versus later.

My first order of business was to find out as much as I could about Sapphire or Jewel Sky, or whatever fucking name, she was using now. *Dead Bitch,* was the new name I planned to give her disloyal ass, and she could just consider me *Karma.* Finding her wouldn't be easy though, especially since the feds knew they were up against, three of the most treacherous women in the world. I had no idea what my sister's plans were, or mine, but eventually they would intersect and come together beautifully. I had to be the boots in the ground in order for this to work, I had to do my research, and planning. Most people would find this boring, but they probably didn't ask questions the way I did.

I had somewhat of a game plan in mind, as I scanned through my father's political favors. Stopping beside the name of the attorney who got me out, after the feds detained me, while they snuck my mother out of town. If I would've been just a few minutes earlier, I could've left that bitch lifeless. It took a hard shaking of my head to center my thoughts, as I reached for my phone to make the call. It probably could've waited until morning, but I wanted to get shit moving. Half a dozen rings brought me a tired man's voice, that was vaguely familiar.

"It's, Freedom Walker," I said, interrupting his tirade about the late hour.

"Uh, wh-what can I do for you, Ms. Walker?" He asked, suddenly wide awake at 4:00 a.m.

"I need to know who was in charge of the feds, guarding my mother, the night she killed my father."

"Uh, well um, that info will be hard to come by be-cause-"

"What I don't want is excuses Mr. Danilson, so save any. I'll be in Chicago soon, when I get there, I expect re-sults," I said, ending the call, before he could get another word in.

I caught my fingers lingering on the screen, right be-fore I hit send for the number I'd dialed unconsciously. I desperately wanted to hear Bone's voice, if only to tell him that none of this was his fault. I could've blamed him, but I wasn't a petty bitch, who needed someone to be mad at. I knew exactly where to direct my anger and hate now. I pushed everything over to one side of the bed, I turned the light out, and laid back down. So many images played on the back of my eye lids, that I doubted I would know sleep as intimately as I wanted, but thankfully, I was wrong.

The area between awake and asleep hit me so sud-denly. I didn't have time to be grateful, and just as quickly, it was ripped away by the sound of squealing tires. This noise was a common occurrence in the hood, so it shouldn't have disturbed me, but being in a foreign environment had my senses on high alert. In seconds I was up, peeking out of the rooms, one window down into the parking lot. I didn't see any police lights in the mid-afternoon sun, or a swat team, but I still found distress outside my window. Luckily, I'd fallen asleep in all my clothes because there was no time to waste. Snatching the door open I stepped outside, ready to let my chopper breath, but the taillights on my new car were fading fast.

"Fuck!" I yelled, moving back into the room, before someone spotted the crazy bitch, with a gun. I couldn't even contemplate the odds of having my car stolen now of all times. Instead I had to figure out what my next move was. Calling Uber was out of the question. Part of me wanted to break down and have a good cry, but all I kept seeing was my father's face, and crying wasn't acceptable. I looked at my phone, it was damn near 2:00 p.m., which meant, I'd slept way past check out. I needed to get on the move, but first I had to check my gut feeling about the random act of my car theft.

After gathering my little bit of shit, I wiped the room clean of my prints with a towel and made my way back to the front desk. Given the time of day, I knew walking in with my AK out wasn't a good idea, which was why I had it in my backpack, the Glock was within reach. One look at the Spanish guy behind the desk, actually had me wishing for the bigger gun back. Before me stood a mufucka at least six-five, two hundred and seventy pounds, with no name tag. He fit every stereo type of the Spanish gang banger you saw on T.V., right down to the tattoos that seemed to cover every inch of him. No wonder no one worried about check out time, the sight of him made you not wanna check in.

"Yes, my car just got stolen, I'm in room 202."

"There's no one in 202, checked out this morning," he replied with a straight face.

"Homie, this ain't how you wanna do this," I warned patiently.

His response was a half-smile, that I could only assume was used to intimidate mufucka's, but it was obvious he'd never met a bitch like me.

"So, is that how you all play it out here, picking on poor, unsuspecting, helpless women?" I asked, feigning emotion, while my right hand slowly went to the pistol under my shirt.

"Listen bitch, ain't nobody got time for your crocodile tears, or sad story. My advice is, that you get the fuck out of here. Unless your car isn't the only thing you wanna lose."

The twinkle in his eye had changed, I could tell he was evaluating me as a piece of pussy now. Just another mistake on his part.

"Where's my car going?" I asked calmly.

Again, I got that half-smirk, but that changed as quickly as the pistol that materialized in my hand.

"Okay, so where's your car?" I asked, smirking myself.

"You, think you're the first bitch to pull a gun on me? You better use it."

Past experiences, had taught me that when a mufucka made a statement like that, he meant it. A reckless homicide wasn't a good look right now, though. In this day and age, everything was digital, recorded, and put all over the internet. Making broad daylight shootings hard to get away with. However, given the obvious illegal activities that took place here, it was unlikely any cameras in here were working. I just needed to get him out of sight. I could feel the smile tugging at the corners of my mouth, as I pulled the trigger, and that made me think of my dad. My shot blew a nice chunk out of his shoulder, causing him to hit the wall behind him, and bellow out in pain.

"Burns, huh?" I asked, coming around the desk to prevent him from scrambling away.

"Let's try this again. Where's. Your. Car?"

"F-fuck you bitch!" He growled through clenched teeth, eyes blazing with murderous intent.

A quick glance around, revealed no one outside being any wiser about what was going on inside. This made my decision easy. Stepping towards the bent over figure in front of me, I pulled the triggers again, and blew the top off his head. With effort, I rolled his dead body over, and searched until I found his keys. Once I had them in hand, I went into the back. As I suspected, I found the camera set up for the entire motel unhooked. Still, I took the CD that was in the computer and put it in my bag for later destruction.

Cool, calm, and collected, I walked back out front in search of the dead man's car. It wasn't until my feet hit the sidewalk, that I realized I was holding a motorcycle key.

Seeing no sign of the bike out front, I circled around the back of the building, where I found a money green Honda CBR 1000, with a helmet to match. Since it was probably stolen, it only seemed fitting that it end up with someone who could appreciate its raw power.

Luckily for me whatever drugs the doctors had given me were still in my system, and I was only feeling slight discomfort. Tucking my pistol and strapping on my backpack, I hopped on my new ride, and got in the wind. I already knew, by car, at normal speed it would take about seven hours to get to Chicago, but I was sliding the bike to a stop in front of the lawyers house a quick four and a half hours later.

The beginnings of dusk, were starting to settle all around me, which meant nightfall was coming. Good judgement dictated, I wait until then to start the party, but every moment wasted, was another opportunity for that bitch to get further away. Scanning the street for signs of foot traffic, or the cops, I pulled my pistol, and stepped to the front door of the nice sized townhouse. As soon as I rung the bell, I heard a woman's voice announce she would get it. The look on her face, when she opened the door to find my gun winking at her, made her quickly say, "Honey, it's for you."

Aryanna

Chapter 6
Destiny

"Yo, I don't know how this bitch, stays way out here in this cold ass weather. But this ain't natural," I said, shivering despite the heavy fur coat Angel's driver had provided, as soon as I stepped off the plane.

"Don't worry, we won't be here long," Sam said, snuggling closer to me in the backseat.

Wrapping my arms around her, I accepted her warmth while appreciating everything she represented. I'm a strong bitch, but it takes a stronger one to check me about my bullshit, and still love me all in the same breath. I'd found that in Black Sam and the last few days helped me to see, she wasn't only what I wanted, but what I needed too. Father God and Free, had always taught us not to need anyone or anything except each other, but Sam, was the exception to that rule.

"Thanks for coming with me," I said, squeezing her tighter.

"Don't you mean for getting you out here," she replied, her words tingling with laughter.

"Whatever bitch," I said, hitting her playfully.

I knew she was joking in a serious way, because I hadn't realized how dependent I'd become on being inebriated all the time. Not drinking or smoking the past few days, had been a mufucka to cope with, but I trusted Sam, when she said it was for the best. I needed to be clear headed, in order to focus on whatever was coming next. Because right now only Free, knew the game plan, and she wasn't telling nobody shit.

"You had any luck finding, Free?" I asked, even though I knew the answer.

"I'm trying babe, but you know your sister is as skilled at going underground as anyone we know. I don't know how she's doing it, either. None of our contacts have heard from her."

I knew Free, wasn't stupid, but this was beyond crazy for her to go off chasing a ghost by herself. We moved as one till death, no exceptions.

"We're here," the driver announced, bringing the Mercedes to a stop in front of a club.

By appearance, you might not have thought it was a club. It was built like a damn castle, but I knew Angel, was out here growing Kamile's empire.

"Damn," Black Sam whispered, when she leaned off me, to look at her surroundings.

Once our door was opened we stepped out, only to be met by two beefy mufuckas, with matching scowls on their faces.

"Great personalities," Black said sarcastically, taking my hand, leading the way behind our escorts.

Once we made it up to the stairs, through the double doors, there was no doubt, this was a strip club. There were five smaller stages, with stripper poles, surrounding a main stage lifted higher than the others. The rest of the room contained plush leather chairs, for the audience, and a full-length bar lined on the far wall in front of us. I could feel my palms start to sweat, at the sight of liquor. But, in the same instant, I felt Sam tighten her grip on my hand, pulling me in the direction we were being led in.

Damn, I loved this woman. I'd learned long ago, a team is only as strong as its weakest link. Where I'm weak she's strong and that's why we worked. We were led down a long dark hallway, until we came to a huge steel door, where the pair in front of us parted and stood on each side of the door. Once we were standing in front of the door, it swung inward, and there sat my second reason for living.

"Being a boss looks good on you bitch, but what's with the body guards, and bullet proof doors?" I asked, letting go of Black Sam's hand, crossing to where Angel stood with open arms.

"It's way different over here than back home, so when you're getting money, you gotta move like the president. Damn bitch, did you forget how to eat or something?" Angel stepped back, looking me over from head to toe.

I knew I had to look rough, wearing a navy blue Black Billionaire sweat suit, with some straight back cornrows, and butter Timbs. It was what it was though, I had my queen, so there was no one left to impress.

"I'm still healthy enough to handle the bad bitch on my arm," I replied, smiling, despite the concern in her hazel eyes.

At the mention of Black Sam, I saw Angel's gaze shift to her, but she didn't speak right away.

"Come, have a seat Sam," I said, keeping my eyes on Angel, trying to gauge what she was thinking.

"What's going on, Black Sam?" Angel asked.

"Just trying to live life outside of prison."

"Naturally that's all of our ambition, but I meant, what the fuck is going on with my sister?" Angel asked, her tone making it clear she was anything but happy.

"Angel chill I'm-"

"I'm not talking to you Destiny. I'm talking to that bad bitch, you keep on your arm. She knows better than to lie to me, but you obviously don't."

"Lie to you? What the fuck have I lied to you about?" I asked, taking a step back, sizing her up, to see how serious she was.

"A lie by omission is still a lie, you know we don't do that shit. It's obvious you've been struggling, I get that in a way nobody else will. But you should've come to me, Destiny. I know Freedom, has kept her distance, now she's run off to God knows where. I'm here though, baby sis, I'm always here," she said softer, opening her arms again.

When I stepped back into her embrace, it felt like a ton of bricks had been lifted, as the tears came in salty waves. Even with Black Sam, by my side these past six months. I'd still felt more alone than I ever had in life, without my sisters. It wasn't until this moment, that I realized how close I'd come to losing myself, since I'd lost my dad and sisters. The only thing I could hope for now, was that some healing could begin. Along with a lot of killing.

"You're my Angel," I mumbled into her chest.

"And you're my Destiny, always," she replied through tears of her own.

We stayed locked in each other's arms a few more moments, until our emotions weren't so raw and exposed. When we were finally separated, I turned to see Black Sam, with tears streaming down her beautiful face.

"Look at your sappy ass," I said, smiling through my own tears, as I moved towards her, giving her a quick hug and kiss.

"So, what's been going on, don't bullshit me either," Angel said.

"It doesn't matter, I'm good now. I promise," I replied, turning back to face her.

I could still read the hesitation and indecisiveness in her eyes, but after a brief pause, she let it go, and retook her seat. We all knew we had bigger shit to worry about now.

"Have you found anything?" Angel asked, turning her attention to Black Sam.

"Nothing. You know like I do that Free, is the one who taught us all the tricks or the trade, so if she doesn't wanna be found she won't be."

"She's fucking trippin', she knows we don't rock like this. We all move or no one does!" Angel said heatedly.

"I know your mad, I feel the same way, but right now we're gonna focus on finding her. I can't lose her too. I – can't," I said, fighting back tears of sorrow and frustration.

"You two know her better than anyone, so what's her next move gonna be?" Black Sam asked.

Her question was met with silence, while we contemplated.

"We know she has to be going after Sapphire, but how will she find her?" Angel asked.

"I've been thinking the same thing. Sam, has checked with anyone we know that could offer tech support. Have you talked to Bone?"

"A few times and he's not himself. I can tell he's trying to be strong for B.J., but he's terrified, he's lost Free. I mean she didn't even hold her son for more than a few moments, then she just fucking unleashed," Angel replied, shaking her head.

"How is our nephew?" I asked.

"Oh God, he's so damn cute! He looks like Dad, Bone, and Free all in one."

"I can't wait to meet him, one day," I said wishfully.

"You will. First we gotta find his crazy ass momma," Angel sighed with frustration.

"If we just had some idea where-." Black Sam's, statement was interrupted by all of our phones going off simultaneously.

I pulled mine out to find a message from Bone, about a mufucka getting his head knocked off somewhere in Kansas. I started to dismiss it, to finish our more important conversation, but I kept reading the message and felt my heart beating quicker.

"Baby-."

"I'm already on it," Sam said, moving quickly around Angel's desk to get at her computer.

"Why does Bone, think this has anything to do with, Free?" Angel asked, moving out of the way for Black Sam.

"Did you not read the whole text message? Somebody reportedly saw a woman fitting Free's general description.

On the second floor of the motel, with a gun out hours before they found dude missing his brain matter," I said.

"Yeah, but that could be anybody in the world. I know he's desperate to find her, just like we are, but we can't start grasping at straws to-"

"He wasn't grasping," Black Sam interjected, stepping back from the laptop.

I was up in a flash and around the desk, to get a look at the screen. Before me was traffic cam footage of a woman riding away from the motel, but you couldn't see her face because of the helmet. None of us needed to see her face, we'd all seen Free, on a bike before.

"Wh-where did you say this was again?" Angel, asked in a strangled whisper.

"Kansas," Black Sam replied.

"Which is exactly how far from, Chicago? I asked.

With a few strokes of the keys Black Sam, had a route picked out and an estimated time of arrival based on the time stamp from the traffic cam footage.

"I can't believe she'd go back there, though." Sam commented.

"She would and she did. Free, is only seeing blood, so whoever you put in front of her will die. The decision is what do we do?" Black Sam asked.

One look at Angel, and I knew we were back to sharing the same brain.

"I'll make the arrangements," she said.

We knew the risks, especially for me, but it didn't matter. I'd ride straight into hell for my sisters. What awaited didn't matter. It was time to get back on U.S. soil and fill it with blood and bodies.

Chapter 7
King Deuce

"Come on homie, don't ask me no dumb questions. Why would I only take over one side of Nashville? When the nigga Monster, laid claim to the whole thing? He's gone, I'm number one now, so we take the entire city, then move on to the next one," I said, passing the lit blunt to the woman next to me, keeping my gaze on the nigga sitting in front of me.

The meeting taking place, was meant to be one to strategize, and plan my next move in the quest to build my empire. Right now, the only problem I was having, was the fact that I didn't have the brightest group of mufuckas to work with. Out of the niggas sitting on my leather sectional across from me. The only person, I felt confident in was the chick sitting beside me. A.I., Du-Dirty, and Tink, were nothing more than Do-boys, which was the only reason I kept them around. But it was times like this, I questioned my own choice of soldiers for this mission.

Now Tabitha, or T.J. as I called her, was a bad bitch of the highest grade. I needed her to make my plans come to-gether. Ideally, I'd want none other than Angel, by my side. But there was no way, I'd put her in harm's way. Once the takeover was complete, Angel would pick from the spoils of war, like a true queen should. Until then, T.J. would play her position, because it was a universal truth that pussy could disarm a man, quicker than anything else.

One look at T.J. and all you saw was an exotic beauty, with a big ass, and matching titties. What very few people knew, was that the thirty-one year-old, American Indian goddess, was more lethal than heroin when it first hit. Be-hind that smile, hid the mind of a maniac, and that gorgeous body only stayed in shape, because of her *MMA* back-ground. I'd ride with her any day, before I would the weak nigga I'd been addressing.

The only reason A.I., was a part of my team was because, he'd shown some loyalty when we'd done a bid for the *TNDOC*. He thought he was a gangster, but the nigga's real name was Ivan. The only thing gangster about him was his understanding of the laws, and how to get around them. Given the fact, that his sexual preference was in question and this could get you killed in prison. He'd used his book smarts, to make him indispensable on the inside.

I didn't care whose dick he was sucking now, or who was fucking him in the ass. I just needed him to secure all of Monster's, legal assets when the time came. I didn't just plan to take the streets over, I was intent on keeping them, the only way to do that, was to keep the money clean.

"Is there a problem?" I asked, wishing like hell Free, Destiny, and Angel, were here to help.

"Nah, n-no problem. I'll get a listing of all the businesses Monster owned through alias, Shell corporations, and family. I'll report back to you," he replied.

"Good, take these two niggas with you," I ordered, pointing at his two silent partners, sitting next to him.

"I-I was wondering if you had time to think about the preposition I made you," A.I., said hesitantly.

For him to be as smart as he was, I couldn't figure out how he didn't understand, in this life you get what you deserve no more, no less. Somehow, this nigga had it in his mind, that once he helped with the hustle takeover, he should be considered to run some of the business. What he didn't understand, was that he wasn't from, or a part of my world, which meant he didn't have a seat at the table. A dog got the scraps, not the main course.

"Yeah, I thought about it, here's my answer," I replied, accepting the blunt back from T.J., as she slowly stood up.

Despite my heart belonging to Angel Walker, I still had to admire the curves on T.J.'s five-six, one hundred eighty-five pound frame, and the way her jean shorts hugged them curves. I saw A.I open his mouth to speak, but before breath could pass his lips, she volted over the coffee table separating us, kicked him hard enough to add two of his teeth to my plush black carpet. I couldn't help smiling with pride, while I hit my blunt, and T.J., calmly walked back around the table, retaking her seat. I might not have been the sharpest knife in the drawer, but he knew it was time to get the fuck out of my apartment, quickly.

"You forgot your teeth!" I called after him, laughing.

A.I. didn't come back for them, but Du-Dirty was kind enough to grab them as him and Tink, made equally quick exits.

"Was it something I said?" T.J. asked innocently, taking the blunt back from me.

"Nah beautiful, I think he was just in a hurry to get back to work. Speaking of which, what do you got going on today?"

"I've got a fight in Houston, Texas in a couple days, so I need to get down there and start training," she replied.

"What are your odds favored at?" I asked, getting up, going to my safe, that was hidden behind the portrait of Malcom X, hanging on my living room wall.

The symbolism of this hiding place was lost on most, but I understood that to secure that bag took a mentality of *'By any means'*. A retina scan unlocked my treasure chest allowing me to pull out one-hundred thousand dollars.

"Odds are four to one, but you should probably bet on one round, I don't think she'll last two," she replied confidently.

Closing the safe, I put the money on the coffee table, and sat back down next to her. A true hustler gets his money any way he can, and betting on T.J., was a sure thing, because she was a fighting mufucka.

"I want you to drop that off to the bookie on your way out," I said.

"Do you need me to stay? I can postpone the fight. Handling this situation is more important and certainly more lucrative."

"Everything is under control. I've got my product moving through both Memphis and Nashville, and the killing that needs to be done is being handle quietly. Once the legit businesses are under my control, I can start cleaning all the money being made, which of course you'll help with," I said, declining the blunt when she offered it to me this time.

"Is that all you need me to help you with?" She asked, putting the blunt in the ashtray, on the table, kneeling in front of me.

I wasn't in business of selling dreams to females. T.J. knew better than most how much I loved women, because we'd had the occasional threesome. She knew there would be no title driven, no matter what we did, which made it easier for some no-strings attached action. The only problem with all this, was that she wasn't Angel, and that's who I wanted.

"You ain't gotta do all that," I said, putting my hand on top of the one she was using to go at my zipper.

"I know I don't have to, but I want to. You don't have to deny yourself a little pleasure, just because you're handling big business now."

Looking down into her beautiful brown eyes, I still felt a slight pull of guilt, because she wasn't my queen. We both knew I was only so strong though, so neither of us was surprised, when I didn't stop her this time from unzipping my jeans. To say she gave good head was an understatement, because she was a connoisseur. I'd seen the strength of her hands, but her touch was gentle, when she wrapped both hands around my shaft, guiding my dick to the back of her throat.

As her lips closed around me, I felt the air get trapped in my lungs, not a breath passed my lips, as she continued taking more of me in her mouth. Her trip back up to the top of my dick was equally slow and painful in the best way. I could see the twinkle of satisfaction dancing in her eyes.

"Damn," I whispered hungrily, giving in, letting my hands find their way into her long, black silky hair, so I could control her speed. Most women would object or insist they knew what they were doing, to get you to let their hair go. T.J. loved proving she really had no gag reflex. Within seconds, I lost myself in the sweet, hot, wetness of her mouth, as she allowed me to fuck her face while she sucked me up with the force of a tornado.

"Y-your gonna make me c-cum," I warned, gripping her hair tighter.

Her response was to use her hand to massage my balls, almost like she was coaxing my organism to arrive sooner. Suddenly, her mouth was no longer devouring my dick, instead her tongue was caressing my balls, as her hand took over by jacking me off.

"T-T.J.! Goddammit." I growled.

Through clenched teeth, seconds before the first drops of cum shot out of me. Before I had a chance to fully enjoy my climax, she had my dick in a death grip that froze my bullets in the chamber.

"Wh-what the fuck?" I panted confused.

"I got this," she replied, not losing her grip as she stood up, using her free hand, to unbutton her shorts.

I opened my mouth to argue, but she'd already pushed her shorts to her ankles, revealing that her pretty pussy and ass weren't covered by panties. Without letting me go, she kicked one leg free, spun around, and straddled me reverse cowgirl style. There were no words from either of us, as she took my dick inch-by-inch inside her tight, wetness, and all thoughts of anything other than this moment were forgotten.

"Fuck me," she ordered, moving up and down purposefully.

My hands immediately went to her plump, juicy ass, as I watched my dick disappear inside her, over and over again. With each stroke it felt like she got wetter and tighter, which made me want to cum again, but I wanted her to cum with me.

"Take the dick! Take it-."

"King Deuce, we got a problem," Greedy said, busting into my apartment unannounced.

Greedy was my eyes and ears on the ground in Nashville, because he was a neutral nigga who was cool with everybody. If he didn't have a damn good reason for interrupting, he wouldn't be cool with me for long though.

"What the fuck are you doing, bruh?" I asked, pissed at the intrusion, but loving the fact that T.J., was still bouncing on my dick.

"It's–it's your mom, homie. She's dead!"

Chapter 8
Angel
Four Days Later

Despite the tragedy, that had more or less run us out of town, it still had been easier getting out of the U.S., than it was getting back in. It had taken us three days in a cargo shipping container, to make it from Russia back into Canada and another day crossing the border into Vermont. We were all tired and filthy, but determined to find Free, before death did.

"We need to get some sleep, before we start the next leg of our journey," Black Sam said, once everyone was seated in the living room of the safe house.

I could feel the fatigue in my bones, now that the fire Lil' Boy built, had sufficiently warmed up the one-story log cabin and thawed me out. I'd thought Russia was bad, but it was obvious winter in this part of the world, was nothing to fuck with either. Thankfully, all the money we'd amassed provided us with the means to move and live comfortably, unlike most fugitives.

"You all can get some sleep, I'm gonna start trying to pick up Free's trail," I replied, pulling out my phone to let Bone know we'd made it safely across.

My communication with him had been off and on due to our travel plans. But I knew Free, had touched down in Chicago, and slaughtered an entire family. I didn't blame her, I wanted revenge too, but there was a way to go about it and this wasn't the way. The fact that the lawyer's family, had been dismembered meant she was after information, and since everyone including the kids had died. It was clear, she didn't get what she was after. That meant she was still hunting.

"We all need to sleep, Angel," Lil' Boy said, sitting next to me on the couch.

Even though, I knew he was right, and he was only telling me this because he cared, it still annoyed me. Instead of jumping down his throat, I got up and found my way to one of the back bedrooms, closing the door behind me. My body yearned for the comfortable looking king size bed in front of me, but I flopped down in the wicker chair beside the door and went back to texting.

Free's little killing spree, was on every major news outlet and all over social media, which fueled my frustration, and annoyance. Because she was drawing heat quicker than Dante's inferno. She was smart enough to know that her actions would throw a net around her and us, but it seemed she didn't care, that worried me. At the rate she was going, this situation would turn into a reckoning that concluded in all of us being dead, instead of simply those that needed to die. We had to stop her before then, or die trying.

"Hey," I said, answering the ringing phone in my hand.

"Where are you?" Bone asked.

I could hear the stress and anxiety in his voice, that pumped even more adrenaline into my veins, because both weren't familiar to me coming from him.

"We're at the cabin. Why, has something else happened?"

"No. Nothing new, I still ain't heard from her yet," he replied dejectedly.

"We'll find her bruh, I promise. You know she's not gonna keep us in the dark, forever."

"I know that, but she's gonna get herself killed, Angel. Trump, has been all over the news talking about the violence in Chicago, with the latest victims being kids, he's actually got mufuckas behind him. They're not gonna try to apprehend her, they're gonna shoot her down like a dog in the street."

I didn't want to face the truth in his statement, even though deep down I knew he was right. Black lives didn't matter anymore now, then they had in the last four hundred plus years. Given what Free, had done the masses would rather see her swinging lifeless from a tree, than in a courtroom where anything could happen. But if they kill her, they'd better damn sure kill us all.

"The cops still don't know who they're looking for, which means we still have a chance to find her first," I replied, hoping to reassure him and myself.

"It's only a matter of time, Angel! We gotta find her before – before…"

I'd never heard so much emotion in Bone's voice before, it was causing a sudden panic to rise within me. I knew without a doubt that the nigga on the other end of this phone was a gangsta. But it was evident losing my sister was the one thing that could and would bring him to his knees. It would destroy all of us and there was no way I could let that happen.

"Just sit tight bruh. We'll be down there as soon as we can, okay?" I told him, projecting a calm I definitely didn't feel.

"Okay. There's something else you need to know, though. It's about King Deuce."

At the mention of Vonte's name I felt something in the pit of my stomach, I couldn't quite describe. In the months I'd spent in exile, he'd crossed my mind a lot. Enough time hadn't passed for me to feel safe contacting him. Based on Bone's statement, it was obvious I should've taken the chance.

"What about, K.D.?" I asked cautiously.

"His mom got killed a few days ago, she was strangled."

"Wh-what, by who?" I asked, feeling sick to my stomach.

I hadn't met his mom, but I knew they were close, and I knew how it felt to lose a parent to unnatural causes.

"I don't know. I haven't talked to him. I just saw it on the news. The cops are saying its gang related, because the numbers five and two were carved into her forehead."

Within seconds, the lightbulb went off in my brain telling me, this was payback for the murder of the big homie Monster, from 5 Deuce Hoover Crips. The beef between him and K.D., had been real until I entered his life in dramatic fashion, but this killing let it be known, the war wasn't over. Shit, if I knew K.D., the real war had just begun.

"Where is he?" I asked, trying not to choke on the guilt, I felt for leaving him here to deal with the fallout by himself.

"Today's the funeral. Listen, I'm only telling you this, so you can call him, but you gotta stay focused on the task at hand. You know Free, is living on borrowed time."

I'd never felt more torn, than I did at this moment, but I knew what my sister would expect of me in this moment.

"I know what I gotta do, just sit tight, and keep my nephew safe. We'll be there in a minute," I said, disconnecting and already mentally making my next move.

I knew the risks of communication via Facebook, but I still pulled up K.D.'s page, to see what I could learn. There were tons of condolences and well wishes. King Deuce had been silent, not offering so much as a thank you, or a fuck you. He was hurt and there was no way I could let him go through that alone. With my mind made up, I got up, and went back into the living room. Where I found Sam, Destiny, Lil Boy, and Big Baby still sitting around the fire.

"I'm going to Tennessee," I announced, picking up my bag with my fake passport, money, and guns in it.

"Wait, you're what? Bitch are you crazy? You can't go down there," Destiny replied quickly.

"I gotta go. Somebody killed K.D.'s mom, it's my fault."

"How the fuck is it your fault? Or your problem? When we've been out of the country," Lil Boy said, standing up.

"Right?" Black Sam chimed in.

"It's my fault because, it's retaliation for the shit that went down in the strip club. It's my problem because K.D. is family. He ain't never left me or my sisters for dead," I replied, looking directly at Destiny, challenging her to call me a liar.

Sure, I'd saved K.D.'s life a time or two, but there wasn't nothing he wouldn't have done for any of us. He'd already proven that to me, by saving my ass when I needed it most.

"K.D. may be like family. But, Freedom, is family. Which is more important to you?" Lil' Boy asked.

The glare I turned on him, should've conveyed how fucked up it was for him to even say some shit like that to me. But he didn't wilt beneath my stare. While it was true Lil' Boy and I had grown closer over these last months. That still didn't give him the right to question my loyalty, or judgement.

"You a bold mufucka, to come out your mouth with some shit like that. I'ma tell you only one time. You better not come at me like that again. Family is family, period. You better hope, I remember that when your ass needs me," I said coldly, heading towards the front door.

"Angel wait," Destiny said, standing up, crossing the room to where I was.

"King Deuce is family and if anybody understands what he's going through its us. All Lil' Boy is trying to say, is that we're back for one reason. Plus, your ass is wanted for escaping from Tennessee's custody. It's suicide to go back sis."

"Just like it would be suicide, for any of you to show your faces in Chicago?" I asked, looking around the room.

As expected, my question was met with silence, because they all knew I was right. Family protected each other and was there for each other regardless of what harm stood in the way. Loyalty couldn't be conditional, or it wasn't authentic, Father God had taught me that.

"So, what about, Free?" Lil' Boy asked.

"It should be easier to find her now. When you do, I'll be there," I replied impatiently, again, heading for the door.

"Hold up, I don't necessarily agree, but you damn sure ain't going anywhere, by yourself," Destiny said, grabbing my arm.

I wasn't used to taking orders from my baby sister, but I knew I'd have to concede this point, or I might never get going.

"Fine, I'll take someone with me." At this declaration Lil' Boy went, picked up his bag, and came to stand beside me.

Ordinarily, he probably would've been my first choice for a list of reasons. However, I had one reason I didn't want him going with me, jealousy. He'd put forth a legit argument about the choice I was making to go to Tennessee. I'd seen something in his eyes, he was trying to keep hidden. I couldn't say, I didn't have feelings for him. I just couldn't let that cloud my judgement, or actions at the moment. I had no idea, what awaited me in the South, but I knew that a dick swinging contest wouldn't help.

"Big Baby, you roll with me," I said, not making eye contact with anyone except my sister.

We were one, so I knew I wouldn't have to explain my choice. This wasn't the time for hand holding and coddling. Our family was at war from all angles, that meant it was all about survival, because death wasn't cute.

Chapter 9
Freedom

"Oh—my—God!"

"No, I'm not God. I'm his daughter and depending on how you answer the next question you might meet my father," I promised, pushing the barrel of my Glock 9mm into her eye socket.

Her fear was as evident, as the shaking beneath the robe, provided by the luxury day spa, and I like that. It fed the growing need inside me. I wanted the world to fear me for what had happened to my father. I wanted them to remember why we weren't to be fucked with.

"My time is short and my patience is shorter Brenda, so let's skip the small talk. You're gonna get up nice and slow, put your fifteen thousand dollar dress back on that saggy ass body, and were gonna take a ride." I instructed calmly.

The use of her first name, added a level of terror to her blue eyes, as it became clear to her, this wasn't a random occurrence. To me that should have been obvious. I didn't know too many bitches who got ran up on, while luxuriating in their seaweed wax in an upscale D.C spa. Today was Brenda Lewis's lucky day, because her husband was no other than assistant F.B.I director, Mark Lewis.

My research showed, they'd been together twenty years, married for fifteen, had one seventeen-year-old daughter, and unlike most men in a position of power, Mark didn't have a mistress. All this brought me to the conclusion, that Mark loved his wife and family. Thus, exposing his weakness, giving me the leverage I needed.

I had hoped to get more info out of my former lawyer, but it turned out, he didn't rub elbows with the right people. I was still mad for getting so caught up in that situation, because had I not killed his whole family the way I did. I wouldn't have had to flee Chicago so quick. I'll be smarter this time.

"Pl-please, if its money you want, just take me to the nearest ATM. I'll give you whatever you want. Just please don't hur-hurt me," she begged, raising her hands straight in the air, like she'd seen done in the movies.

Given the avocado mask she was sporting it was also comical, but I was beyond laughter at this point in my life.

"Bitch get up and stop insulting my mafucking intelligence. We both know, I'm not here about no money, get dressed," I said, cocking the hammer on my pistol to prevent further useless commentary.

I didn't move my gun from her eye socket, until she was standing, then I took a small step back, allowing her to disrobe, and put her Gucci dress back on. I knew I couldn't exactly walk out the front door with her at gun point, but my bluff game was phenomenal, and I had a plan. Once she was dressed, I tucked my gun in the small of my back and pulled out my phone.

"Listen carefully, I don't wanna repeat myself. We're gonna walk out of here real cool and get in that silver Maserati, you've got parked out front. If you can do that without any problems, then the men I have watching your daughter won't rape and kill her. If not..."

I let the threat hang in the air as I turned my phone towards her, so she could see the picture of her daughter, laughing with her friends at her private school in the suburbs of Virginia. Her tears came instantly, making tracks of avocado, puddled at her chin waiting to fall. As a mother myself, I knew I should've felt bad about threatening or harming kids, but a conscience wasn't a luxury I could afford, nor did I want, I wanted blood.

"Wipe your face and let's go," I ordered, tossing her one of the plush complementary towels the spa provided.

Even with the avocado gone the tears still came, but she gathered her composure, as quickly as she did her purse. I kept my eyes peeled for any threats or wanna-be heroes, as we made our way out front, into her car. I hated to leave my bike, but it was probably time to get rid of it anyway, considering it still had Kansas plates. In this city, I had no illusions that it would remain idle long, which was why I'd made sure to wipe it down and leave the key in the ignition. Christmas would come early for whatever lucky mufucka happened upon it.

Before accosting Brenda at the spa, I'd mapped out the quickest route back to her family townhouse, in the upscale Georgetown neighborhood of D.C., and made sure to give her specific directions to avoid detours for help. Within twenty minutes, we were pulling up out front, making our way inside. Given the mid-afternoon hour, I knew we had some time to kill until her husband arrived.

I planned to use that time to set the stage for the main event. Once we were inside, with the door locked and the alarm reset. I led the still silently crying, woman into the kitchen, and made her sit down.

"You're probably wondering what this is all about, huh?" I asked, sitting across from her.

I could tell she was too upset to give a verbal response, but I did notice a slight shaking of her head.

"It's simple really. Your husband and his boss, allowed my mother to murder my father, and get away with it. Now everyone has to answer for that," I said matter-of-factly.

"He-he wouldn't do that. My husband is an honest man," she protested, shaking her head negatively.

"Honest men make mistakes, but we both know that Mark's honesty and integrity only goes so far, because he works for a system that's broken and corrupt."

"Y-you can't blame him for the flaws in the government, please-"

"No, but I can blame him for turning a blind eye to murder," I said heatedly.

"Mark wouldn't do that, I know he wouldn't."

"So, why hasn't there been an arrest made? They know who gunned down my father, they're still protecting that bitch! She's the one that deserved to die, not Father God!" At the mention of my dad's legendary name, she flinched. That told me despite policy good ole Mark, must've brought his work home with him.

"I can tell you've heard of my dad," I said, watching her closely.

"N-no I-."

"Bitch, don't lie to me," I warned, pulling my gun back out, pointing it at her face.

"I only k-know what was on the news, about his escape, and his killing in Chicago. So-."

"So, what? That means he deserved to die, is that it?!" I yelled, hopping up out of my seat, pounding the table before she could move an inch.

"No, I-"

She didn't get to finish her sentence, before I slammed the butt of my pistol in her mouth, making her choke on three of her teeth. I could see her pleading for mercy with her eyes, but I couldn't stop myself, from hitting her repeatedly, until she lost consciousness. My breath came in great gasps, as I stood over her motionless body at my feet. I felt a little better.

She primarily didn't know shit anyway. I only needed to keep her alive long enough to make her husband talk. I knew just the thing to expedite this process.

After tucking my gun back into the waist of my jeans, I picked her up off the floor and carried her into the living room. After I had her stretched out on the couch, I went back for her purse, where I found her cellphone.

Once I found her husband's number, I quickly pushed the phone under her dress, and took a picture of her pussy. Of course, the picture wasn't very good. I wasn't about to play with this bitch, but it would get the job done, of enticing her man home for an afternoon quickie. I had no idea how raunchy they got in the bedroom, so I accompanied the picture with a text, that said come fuck me, and sent it to him.

Within minutes, I was looking at the horrific sight of an uncircumcised *white* penis, saying it would be there in an hour. That didn't leave me a lot of time to set the scene. I'd have to rely on what I needed being somewhere in this house. I pulled a pair of black latex gloves from my pocket, I slipped them on and ran for the stairs leading to the second floor. It took two wrong doors, before I found their bedroom.

I found what I needed almost immediately in their walk-in closet. My discovery came in the form of an old school treasure chest. That certainly explained how they'd stayed married, so long. Inside were all the props needed to shoot *Fifty-Shades Darker* in 3D, but the whips, and dildos didn't interest me. I grabbed two pair of furry handcuffs and a ball gag, I headed back downstairs.

After quickly rolling Brenda over, handcuffing her hands behind her. I put the ball gag in her mouth and secured it tightly. Even though she was unconscious. I still felt better with her unable to scream or fight back and I still had more shit to gather. In the basement, I found what I needed at the work station of whoever was leading the remodeling project. After grabbing a nail gun and some plastic, I went back upstairs to the still unconscious Brenda.

It was times like this, when I regretted my decision to operate on my own. What I had to do next, would go faster with more hands-on deck. I'd do what I had to do though. It took almost the whole hour laying out plastic at Brenda's feet. After nailing her to her living room wall. But, I finally had the crucifix scene set. Fifteen minutes, later I heard the deactivation of the alarm as a tall, slender, brown haired white man hurried into the house.

"Oh lover!" He sang out, heading right past the living room, towards the stairs.

"We're in here," I said, just above a whisper.

Instantly the direction of his footsteps changed, allowing me to hear his arrival, before I saw him rounding the corner. With the drapes closed and the lighting dim, I knew it would take a minute for his eyes to adjust. When they did, what he saw froze the smile on his face.

"Will you make her pay for your sins, Mark?" I asked, getting up from my seat, stepping into his view. I made sure he saw my pistol, so he didn't get any ideas.

"Wh-what the fuck is this? Who are you?" He asked weakly.

"You know exactly who I am, especially since you're honoring what's left of my family. I'll refresh your memory though," I offered, stepping up beside his wife.

It had been my intention for him to see the pistol in my left hand. I knew he'd never pay attention to the blade in my right hand.

"I wouldn't make any sudden moves," I told Brenda, putting the tip of the razor blade in my right hand, below her belly button on her pelvic bone.

"My name is Freedom Walker," I said, slicing upwards into her stomach slowly, amid her muffled screams.

Out of the corner of my eye, I saw an unconscious flinch from Mark, but leveling my pistol at him ceased any reoccurrences.

"Please, I don't understand, please!" He insisted desperately, dropping to his knees.

"Sure, you do Mark, my dad was none other than Jonathan Walker, a.k.a Father God. You let my mother kill him. A mother, by the way, that was supposedly murdered years ago. But, who you really hid, while you built a RICO case against the Black Guerilla family. All that's water under the bridge now, because you're gonna make it right by telling me where my mother is."

"I-I don't know where-"

I interrupted his lie, by cutting deeper into his wife's stomach, dragging the razor blade higher.

"Please! Okay please, I can find out! Just give me some time!" He begged.

"You have five minutes," I replied seriously.

With trembling hands, he pulled his phone from his pocket and started tapping a mile a minute. I stepped away from Brenda, long enough to make sure he wasn't sending no S.O.S. messages, once I was satisfied I went back to my artistic expression.

"Don't hurt her," he cried out, almost historically when he saw my fingers going back towards the razor blade.

"Focus on getting me what I want," I advised.

I'd barely got to rip through more flesh, before he was scrambling to my side, showing me the screen of his phone. It was obvious his security clearance was only parallel to one. Because based on the flashing red arrows, I was looking at a file that didn't exist. I made sure not to be distracted, by what was in front of me. I'd read it soon enough, once I was done with the Lewis's.

"Sit the phone on the coffee table and back up," I instructed.

Of course, he didn't hesitate to follow my instructions, but I still shot him in both knee caps. His screams were as beautiful as the old school R&B's my dad used to listen to, that made me smile. Turning my attention back to Brenda, I slit her stomach completely open, stepping back just in time to avoid all the guts and intestines that fell to the plastic at her feet.

The look on Mark's face, when he saw his wife inside out, made me feel a little better. Seeing him crawling and hopping around in her fluids, trying in vain to put her back together, made me smile bigger. Pulling out my phone, I made a long overdue call.

Aryanna

"Hey, I just wanted to let you know, I'm okay. I'll be home soon," I said, squeezing the trigger twice, adding Mark's brains to his wife's bowels.

Chapter 10
Destiny

The silence that followed Angel and Big Baby's, exit hung thick in the air for another hour before anyone spoke again.

"I ain't trippin,'" Lil' Boy said, doing exactly that by answering a question no one asked.

I could feel Sam about to comment, but I grabbed her thigh, shaking my head at her.

"She's just mad because I spoke the truth that's all," he said, continuing his one on one dialogue.

I knew Lil' Boy was right to a certain point, but he was overlooking his own actions in this scenario. Anyone who looked at him could tell, he was falling faster each day. He should've known by now not to smother Angel, so I kept my two cents to myself.

"Come on," I said, taking Black Sam, by the hand, leading her to our bedroom.

Once I'd gone back for our bags, I paused in the middle of the floor, with my hands on my hips, staring at Sam.

"Why are you giving me that look?" She asked, without turning to look at me.

"You know why, were you really about to say some shit that would've hurt Lil' Boy?"

"Nooo," she replied slowly and unconvincingly. "I was just gonna tell him the truth because-."

"And you don't think that would've hurt him a little bit," I asked sarcastically.

I knew Black Sam wasn't really mean to people, but she has a habit of brutal honesty, with the emphasis on the word *brutal*. The look of embarrassment on her face now, would make you believe in her innocence, with regard to malicious intent, though sweet, still somewhat naive.

"I didn't mean to-."

"I know baby," I said, opening my arms wide for her to step into them.

My kisses were meant to be those of comfort, but hers were ones I recognized as hunger immediately. Before I knew it, she had my tank top pushed over my head and my incredibly sensitive nipples were throbbing in between her fingertips.

"Uh, ba-baby I thought sleep-"

"We'll sleep when we're done," she insisted, pushing me down on top of the queen-sized mattress.

It was in me to argue just on principle alone, but she already had my pants and panties, around my knee's while her fingers seduced my clit. Just her touch had the need in me screaming, despite my efforts to play it cool. We'd reconciled our differences on a couple occasions since our big disagreement, but this felt different. Before my back got comfortable on the bed, she had it arching with the work her two fingers were doing inside me. I damn sure wasn't about to complain though.

"Oh fuck!" I cried out, once she found my G-spot, and applied pressure to it.

She was merciless using both tongue and fingers in tandem, until I renowned my God to worship only her. After my second orgasm I tried to back away, but she had me in some type of scorpion death grip, that had my toes poppin.

"Holy-holy-oh-fuck! Holy fuck!" I rambled repeatedly, as my third orgasm found me and tried to drown me in its waves.

My ears were ringing so loudly, they didn't even register the phone, but Lil' Boy beating on my door got the message through.

"I'll-be-right-there!" I yelled breathlessly.

I grabbed ahold of Sam's face, pushing it deeper into my soaking wet pussy. My baby didn't need any further encouragement because she had the storm rebuilding in me quickly.

"Destiny it's important!" Lil' Boy hollered, from outside the bedroom door.

"I kn-know!" I yelled back, gripping the head between my thighs tighter while she sucked my clit.

"Hurry!" I panted, hoping Lil' Boy would take a hint. I should've known better.

"It's about Free, she finally made contact," he yelled through the door, successfully killing the whole mood.

Instantly Black Sam froze, then backed up, so she could look up at me. The sight of her covered in my pussy juices and cum was turning me on even more, but the look in her eyes, said we needed to take this seriously.

"Two more minutes, mufucka couldn't wait two more goddamn minutes!" I mumbled, pissed, getting up off the bed to open the door.

"Your eyes better not even think about wandering nigga. They better stay glued to my face. Say what you know and bounce," I ordered seriously.

It was obvious he was having the fight of his life, right before my eyes. It took great effort for him not to look at my naked body. I knew I was thicker than a Clydesdale, but it was a smart decision for Lil Boy, to keep his eyes locked on mine.

"Fr-Free called Bone and said she was alright, then she fired two shots, and hung up."

"Where did the call come from?" I asked.

"Bone sent you and Black Sam, the number, when you didn't respond immediately. I was told to come get you."

"Okay, we'll get on top of it," I replied, closing the door, just as he lost the battle of self-control.

I wasn't surprised to turn around and find Sam already at work on her laptop. But, the fact that she was fully dressed, surprised me.

"Uh, damn Clark Kent, you ain't have to get dressed so fast," I said, slightly offended.

"Aw baby, you were so caught up in the whirlwind, you never got around to undressing me."

My mouth flew open to protest the bullshit, but I quickly realized she was right. From that point my righteous indignation turned to embarrassment, as I made my way towards her, with my head down to hide my sheepish smile.

"It's ok, I still love you," she said, once I reached the side of the bed closest to her.

Since she was the definition of technical support there was nothing I could really help her with except for one thing.

"You know we don't have time," she protested weakly, allowing me to lay her down, without interrupting her work.

Next, I made quick work of her jeans, but I only managed to get her panties to the side, before my tongue found her sweetest secrets. Her whole body tensed, which caused her to hit the wrong keys on the keyboard and cuss, but it made me smile.

"Baby we don't have-have time," she moaned, opening her legs wider, typing even slower than before.

"Shhhh," I breathed right against her pussy lips, knowing how the vibration would make her shiver.

I was rewarded for my efforts with another curse, when she hit the wrong key, but still my onslaught continued. I felt her body opening to me. Any other bitch I knew would've taken some serious offense, when she positioned the laptop on top of my head, but in this moment, we we're the definition of multitasking.

"Call came from, mmph-from Washing-Washington, D.C.," she managed to pant, between my licks.

What she said though only strengthened our suspicions that Free, would go after anybody anywhere to settle this. What it seemed like my big sister didn't know, was that there would never be enough killing to erase the hate and hurt we all felt.

"Victims?" I asked in between licks.

"N-nothing reported yet," she replied, moving her laptop aside finally, holding onto my head the way I'd done hers.

We knew just what each other liked, so now that I had her undivided attention, I could hear her body's song serenading.

"B-baby just one," she pleaded, with regards to how many orgasms she was allowed to have.

Most women were happy getting only one, but Sam's statement was made because, she knew I'd make her beg for hours before I stopped if we had time.

"Deal," I said, pushing my thumb inside her tight asshole, while my mouth went back to feasting. Within seconds, the floodgates opened, and cum gushed into my mouth sweeter than any kool-aid.

"You know I hate to eat and run but-," I said, regretfully sliding from between her still trembling legs in search of my clothes.

"It's o-okay, just give me a minute, I'll join you," she panted with a sweet smile of satisfaction all over her face.

As much as I liked admiring my handy work, I kept getting dressed. My mind already switching gears to catching up with Free. If she was in D.C., it was a safe bet she was going after whoever had answers in the F.B.I, and they weren't known for talking. We were 'bout to ask them in a different way, though. Once I had my clothes on, I grabbed our bag of necessities, to make sure we would have what we needed for the next part of the trip.

"Come on bae, move," I said, checking all the guns, making sure mags and extra mags were full.

"I'm moving, I'm moving." It was still another two minutes, before her words actually led to actions. But that gave me time to finish the weapon part of the inventory.

"You know it's about time to get more clothes, right?" She asked, pulling her panties up.

It saved time and space, traveling as light as possible, when you're on the run. But even more in our case, because we had to be ready to flee the country at the drop of a dime. The problem with that was, we'd been wearing what we had for more than a day and we were already on the move again. Basically, my bitch was letting me know, she was too bad and bougie for any more bullshit.

"Yea baby I know, we'll take care of that, I promise. Right now, can you just squeeze your tight ass back in them jeans," I said, slapping her lovingly on her big ole juicy booty.

After wiggling it at me, she did what I asked, before she started shutting her laptop off, and putting it away. Once I had our bag with everything we'd need for the immediate future secured. I went out into the living room expecting to find Lil' Boy pacing, but instead I found him sitting on the couch staring at his phone.

"Bruh, you ready?" I asked, somewhat confused.

"Yo, she's really fuckin trippin," he said, in obvious disbelief.

"What, who?"

"Your sister. I called to let her and my brother know what was going on and tell them they should come back or meet us. She just say's call if we need them and hangs up." The expression on his face, definitely matched the disbelief in his tone. I probably would've felt bad for him if I had the time.

"Bruh, you know I fuck with you, but we got too much going on for this soap opera-love story type shit," I replied honestly.

"Soap opera – love story? What the fuck you talking 'bout sis, I-."

"Check it, any mufucka with eyes can see that these last six months have brought you and my sister closer. But, you're about to fuck that up. You know Angel bruh, so if anybody knows what to do to turn her off it'll be you. You're making shit way too complicated, when all you gotta do, is be the same nigga you've always been. Then you niggas wonder why you're only good for one thing," I said, shaking my head, while heading for the front door to put my bag in the truck.

When I walked back into the cabin, I expected Lil' Boy to finally be moving, but this nigga was in the same damn spot!

"Yo, you interrupted one of the best orgasms I ever had in my life. Now you think we got time for you to be on your tender dick shit? Man get your soft ass in the truck," I demanded, headed to the bedroom to give Black Sam, the same speech if she wasn't ready.

Luckily for her ass, she was around the corner trying to stifle her laughter.

"Shut up and come on," I whispered, taking her hand, leading her outside.

"And you were worried about me hurting his feelings," she said, climbing into the front seat beside me.

"Smartass," I retorted.

I was a little mad at myself for going so hard on him, but he was no good to me, or any of us on some sucka for love shit. It took a couple minutes for him to finally make it to the truck. When he did his face was an unreadable mask of stone. Thankfully Black Sam, turned on some music, so the awkward silence was avoided, but the emotion was still heavy as I pointed the truck south.

"What's the plan when we get to D.C.?" Sam asked, leaning close to me, so she could whisper into my ear.

"That depends on whether or not you can pinpoint Free's exact location," I replied.

Accepting her challenge, Black Sam, pulled her laptop back out and went to work. I had the upmost confidence in her skills. It was evident Free, was ready to bring us into the equation, or she wouldn't have contacted Bone. She had no way of knowing we were all back in the country, but she knew we'd all need to be a part of this thing in order for it to be truly over.

"Oh-shit," Sam mumbled.

"What?" I asked, immediately shutting the music off.

"Uh, there was a disturbance at the Assistant F.B.I director's house, but it seems like the media is being kept in the dark about the details."

"Okay, I know that won't stop you from finding out what the fuck happened," I said, getting a bad feeling in the pit of my stomach.

"I'm on it, I'm on it," she replied, as her fingers flew over the keys rapidly. A look in the rear-view mirror, told me Lil' Boy was thinking the same thing I was. We knew this wasn't a coincidence, it was obvious Free, was on her Al Capone, shit for real this time. But we'd get on it with her, because everyone who had a hand in my father's death needed killing.

"Oh, God, it's bad babe. Really, really bad," Black Sam said softly.

"Just tell me."

"I'll show you," she replied, turning the laptop screen my way.

Quickly, I pulled over on the little dirt road I'd been navigating and gave the screen my full focus. I could tell by Free's movements and lack of disguise, it hadn't crossed her mind that the house she was in had cameras, or she really didn't give a fuck. Either way I was looking at my big sister, do what she did best, what I saw only left one conclusion.

"They're gonna kill her."

Chapter 11
King Deuce

"I'm so sorry for your loss, Vontae."

I accepted the little black lady's condolences, the same way I had all the others before her, with a slight handshake and head nod. It wasn't like I doubted her sincerity, or anyone else's who'd come to pay their respects to my beautiful mother. I just didn't trust my voice anymore, now than I had at the gravesite service. God only gave us one mother. I cherished mine, no matter how fucked up I'd chosen to live my life.

I couldn't deny the massive guilt I felt though, because she'd been taken for decisions I'd made. That was something I had to live with for however long I lived. I deserved that pain a million times over, in fact I embraced it. I fully intended to use it to turn the world to the ground in the name of, Ms. Shirley Maddox.

First, I just had to make it through the rest of this day. Even though it was custom for all the family to gather at the house of the deceased, share food and memories. I wanted to be anywhere except here in my mother's living room. Based on the looks I'd been getting all day from various family members. I'd say they wanted my black ass somewhere else, too. Maybe it was the fact that I'd came with some goods in tow, including T.J., but I couldn't apologize for that.

I didn't put it past niggas to move on me while I was grieving. Once upon a time, I'd have thought a mufucka wouldn't dare, because I ran Memphis. But the fact that my mother was gone, proved no line wouldn't be crossed. Niggas was gonna learn real soon, that I felt the exact same way.

"Just breathe," T.J. said, coming to stand next to me in the corner of the living room, I was content to occupy.

"Trying to," I murmured, keeping my eyes on everyone moving throughout the house.

T.J. had been the only one I'd allowed inside with me, so I wouldn't further offend the family, that already hated me. It was almost dark outside, and really that was all I was waiting on to make my exit. Tonight, and every night after, the streets would bleed. I was gonna see to it personally.

"What is it?" I asked, noticing T.J. pull her phone from her pocket.

"It would seem you've got an unexpected visitor outside, it's making your homies nervous," The last thing I needed right now was a goddamn shootout on my mother's front lawn, so whoever was outside had better not be on no bullshit.

"Come on," I said, leading the way out the front door, down the porch steps.

My niggas had the whole street blocked off from top to bottom, so I was slightly surprised to see the all black hummer idling at the curb. That surprise turned into absolute shock, when she stepped down from the passenger side.

"What the fuck?" I asked, closing the distance between us, while scanning the street for any type of law enforcement.

"I came as soon as I heard, I'm so sorry K.D.," Angel said, coming towards me, wrapping her arms around me.

I couldn't explain the emotions shooting through me at the moment, shit, I could barely breathe! All I knew was that, I'd never been happier to see anyone in all my life.

"Y-you're really here? Angel, what the fuck are you *doing* here?" I asked, squeezing her tighter for proof that I wasn't imagining shit.

"Where else would I be? We're family."

There was so much I wanted to say, but the fight with the tears in my throat was real right, so all I could do was hold onto her. We stayed locked like that until T.J., not so subtly cleared her throat. Stepping back, I looked down into Angel's beautiful face, wanting to kiss her, but knew now wasn't the time for all that.

"T.J. this is-"

"Angel Walker, one of the notorious, Walker sisters," T.J. interrupted and concluded.

Angel, never took her eyes away from mine, but I could tell she hadn't missed T.J.'s tone, or the disapproval. T.J. was a bad bitch and definitely formidable in the danger department, but Angel, was on another level that few bitches got to.

"I see now why the homies were nervous, you've got one of America's Most Wanted, on your doorstep," T.J. said sarcastically.

"Give us a minute," I said, giving T.J. a look that didn't allow for further comment or question.

"Nice girl, obviously, she knows my name, but not how quickly she can get fucked up," Angel said, once T.J. had walked back inside.

"Fuck all that, what are you doing in the country? And you come down here of all places?"

"That's a conversation for later. Right now, I need to know how you're holding up," she replied.

The look of concern she was giving me was so piercing. I had to look away, until I could pull my emotions together. Vulnerability wasn't something I was used to and Angel was the first woman to ever see me off my square.

"I'm-well, if anyone knows how I am, it's you," I replied softly.

Now it was her turn to look away, but her eyes still shined bright with unshed tears. No amount of beauty could hide the struggles she'd been through. Even though I'd never known in the beginning. The Walker sisters, kept their emotions in check because they refused to let the streets exploit them. I would need coaching on how to do the same.

"As happy as I am to see you. We can't stand out here like this. I don't put it pass the law, to have somebody doing surveillance on me," I said, scanning the street again for anything out of the ordinary.

"Get in," she instructed, turning, and going back towards the still idling hummer.

A brief look back at my mother's house revealed T.J. standing in the window watching, and just over her shoulder another disapproving family member, staring a hole through me. I pulled my phone from my suit pocket, I quickly dialed a number.

"We're on the move, I'm in the black hummer," I said, turning and following Angel.

I heard T.J. calling my name just as the door shut, but we pulled away from the curb before she could make it down the steps.

"Hope she got her bus pass," Angel said, laughing softly.

Despite the day and the mood, I actually found myself smiling slightly. There really were no substitutes for the bad bitch riding shotgun right now, I had to thank God for that.

"Where we going?" She asked.

"Well considering that your ass is hotter than fish grease, and I'm in the middle of a war, I guess we better head to one of my safe houses."

"Shoot the info to the trucks GPS," she instructed.

I did what she said and twenty minutes later, Big Baby was gliding the hummer to a stop in front of a little two-story house on a dead-end street. Once the six trucks packed with my homies pulled up and everybody got out I did the same.

"Damn Mr. President," Angel said, after getting a look at the squad assembled around us.

"I'm taking no chances, come on." I said, leading the way up the sidewalk, into the house.

On the outside, it looked like every other house on the block, maybe even a little more decried and rundown. Inside I had it laid out with the most comfortable furnishings, and technology money could buy. My neighbors, had no idea the whole block was under my constant surveillance, but they'd appreciate it if shit hit the fan.

"Nice spot, a lot better than the last spot you took me to," Angel commented, looking around at the plush, navy-blue, leather couch and eighty-inch big screen T.V., that occupied the living room.

"Yeah, a nigga is moving up in the world. You want a drink?"

"I'm sure you need quite a few, so let's get to it," she replied, flopping down on the couch, next to Big Baby.

I kept the kitchen stocked with good liquor, and after grabbing two bottles of strawberry Cîroc, I joined them in the living room.

"I'm sorry about your pops," I said, passing her a bottle.

"And I'm sorry about your mom."

Both of us, cracked the seal on our bottles, and took long drinks for those we'd lost. I had no idea how to deal with all the pain and anger I felt, but I was hoping the liquor would numb it, if only for a little while.

"So, what are we doing here, Angel? Not that I'm not glad to see you."

"It's a long story. But the short version is that, Free, done lost her damn mind."

"How so?" I asked, taking another drink.

"Well once she had the baby she-."

"Whoa, whoa, hold the fuck up! Free, had a baby? When the fuck did *that* shit go down?" I asked in disbelief.

I mean, there was no doubt that Free, was a woman, and a sexy one at that. But her having a kid, seemed like some twilight zone shit.

"Yeah, her and Bone, had a little boy. There's a lot you don't know, so let me catch you up real quick."

An hour later, I was still sitting in the same spot with my mouth wide the fuck open, not remembering the last time I'd taken a drink from the almost full bottle.

"I don't know what's more unbelievable, everything that happened since we got locked up that night, or the fact that you three have been apart for so long," I said, shaking my head slowly.

"It's beyond crazy," she replied, taking a drink.

Even though she didn't wear her heart on her sleeve, I could tell she was as emotionally drained as I was. That made me respect her more, because in all that chaos she was living through, she still dropped everything to come be by my side. That was loyalty of another kind.

"So-what do you know about what happened to your mom?" She asked softly.

Now I did take a drink, as my reality once again, threatened to crush my skull by crashing down on me. Out of the corner of my eye, I saw her give Big Baby a nod, to which he got up, and made his way outside. I knew she hadn't done that because she didn't trust him, but because of how sensitive the topic of conversation was. Just another testament of how special she really was.

"I got every man under my control looking for answers, but we both know why it happened. My takeover has been anything, but smooth. I thought I had everything taken care of, though," I said, taking another drink to ease the ache in my chest.

Suddenly the bottle was removed from my hand and Angel, was taking my face in her hands.

"I'm *so sorry* Vontae, I shouldn't have just left you, like that."

"It wasn't your-"

I couldn't get the post of my sentence out, because her lips were on mine, and our tongues were comparing strawberry Cîroc. The number of times, I'd envisioned this moment was too many to count. I still couldn't believe this shit was actually happening. Yet part of me was screaming that it couldn't happen, at least not like this.

"Wait-wait," I said, gently pushing her back.

"What?"

"Angel you know I fuck with you. Ever since that night you got shot and saved my life, I been feeling something different for you. I decided once I got out to build an empire for you to rule beside me because you *are* that queen that every real nigga needs."

"Okay, so what's the problem?" She asked, clearly confused by my actions.

"The problem is, I don't want you in a drunken fog. And I don't want you, because you feel guilty about my mom dying. I want you-"

"Shhh, you're overthinking this. First of all, I'm not drunk, and you should be able to look at me, and see that. More importantly, you should know me well enough to know, I wouldn't make this decision about sex lightly, or out of guilt. I want to be with you this way, because it's what I want and need. Because even though you've never said it, you've *proven,* you've got real love for me, and right now love needs to override all else for once. What we do, this life we live, is full of some ugly shit. We both know it's getting ready to get uglier. This moment right here can be beautiful, though."

I'd kick game at a lot of women and sold more dreams than I had dope. But I'd *never* met anyone, like the woman sitting beside me. There was nothing more I could say, it was all about action now. Standing up, I took her hands, and led her in the back to the master bedroom. I hadn't bothered with a lot of decoration in there, but right now. I was damn sure glad, I'd sprung for the California king-sized bed in front of us.

"Are you sure?" I asked, looking first at the bed, then back at her.

Her response was to push me back on the bed, where I was forced to watch her slowly undress. I'd purposefully, never been in the club when Angel, danced. I could tell how bad her body was with clothes on, I didn't want that temptation. Laying there now, I was completely transfixed. I realized I'd had no *idea* how gorgeous her body really was. By the time, she was completely naked, my dick was so hard it hurt, and I was terrified, if she touched me I'd cum instantly.

"Oh lord," I mumbled.

Surprisingly, she blushed hard enough for her entire body to take on a warm glow that only intensified her sexy.

"Are you gonna lay there in that suit? She asked, seductively.

I was faster than Superman, with my movements to get my clothes off, then I did something I rarely do. Reaching in my nightstand, I grabbed a condom, and tore it open, preparing to put it on.

"Hold on, I got that," she said, climbing on the bed, taking it from me.

I couldn't breathe when she took my dick in her hand. All I could do was pray, it wasn't over before it started. Her touch was soft, yet, firm like she knew what she wanted.

"I d-don't wanna hurt you," I said, breathlessly, as she worked the condom down my dick in a slow deliberate way.

"Don't worry, I can handle it."

I don't know what I intended to say, when I opened my mouth again. At the moment she was on top of me, rubbing my dick back and forth across her pussy lips, and I was lost. Immediately my hands went to her waist, suspending her in the air, while she slowly eased down on me. From the moment, the head of my dick penetrated her I could feel us both throbbing, like racing heartbeats. Never had I known anyone, so wet and tight. I wanted to lose myself in the moment, but I kept a close watch on her face, to make sure I wasn't causing her any pain. Suddenly, she slammed down on me, taking the air from both our lungs.

"Angel!" I gasped, holding onto her tighter.

"It's okay, I got this," she replied, moving steadily, and taking more dick with each stroke, until I was completely inside her.

From there I was lost to her. Her moans of passion, were so soft and sensual. Her pussy was so wet, I could hear the suction with each stroke.

"S-slow down bae," I pleaded.

Her response was to smile, as she put her hands on my chest, and rode me with blind determination. I could see the hunger and need clearly mirrored in her beautiful brown eyes, and I knew I'd better fuck or get fucked. When I lifted my hips into her downward motion, I saw the shock waves written all over her face, but that quickly translated into motivation.

"B-baby you gotta s-slow down, I'ma cum!" I churned, holding on for dear life.

"G-good, m-m-me too!" She panted, moving faster.

I tried my best to hold out, but even with the condom on, I felt her pussy spasm right before it released her juices over me, taking me over the edge with her. It was a full five minutes before I could catch my breath, but I still had no words. As I held her tightly to my chest and relished in her heart beating hard with mine.

"You okay?" She asked.

"I should be asking you that, I mean it was your first time."

"I know, but shit the way you came. I thought it might've been yours too," she replied, laughing softly.

"I'm too happy to be embarrassed, just know you're gonna pay for that comment with your, smartass."

"You promise?" She asked, in that sultry tone, that made the hair on my neck raise up.

It also had the dick still buried inside her raising a little too. Just as I was preparing to prove myself, her phone started ringing, and it wouldn't stop.

"You need to get that?" I asked.

"I don't wanna move, especially if it doesn't involve moving on what's inside me. But, I guess I should," she replied, climbing off me reluctantly.

Once she had the phone out and up to her ear, I could feel her whole mood shift. I knew whoever was on the other end, wasn't saying anything she wanted to hear.

"I'm on my way," she finally said, before disconnecting the call.

"What is it?" I asked.

"Free."

"Okay, well I'm coming with you then. There's no way I'ma let you all handle this shit alone," I said, getting up, putting my clothes on.

"That's sweet, but you can't, it's gone too far now."

"What the fuck does that mean? After what just happened, how could you-."

"Free is on camera killing the Assistant director of the F.B.I and his wife. There's no coming back from this, it's kill or be killed, and that goes for *all* of us."

Hearing this declaration, froze my argument in my throat because, I knew she was right. Some shit you could run from, but not this. Knowing this only left one decision for me.

"No arguments, I'm coming."

Chapter 12
Freedom

Three Days Later

"Now in national news, the manhunt is still on for the woman responsible for the murders of Assistant, F.B.I Director Mark Lewis, and his beloved wife of twenty years, Brenda. It's been almost three days now since Freedom Walker, seen here in this edited video, brutally butchered the couple in their D.C home, but the authorities still have no motive for the heinous crime. As you may well know, Freedom Walker, is the daughter of the notorious crime lord Johnathan 'Father God' Walker, of the Black Guerilla family. Who was gunned down by F.B.I agents, a little more than six months ago.

"Speculation continues to swirl about, Freedom Walker's, actions being blatant retaliation for her father's death, but so far F.B.I Director William Ennius, has yet to confirm this. The Director did however, issue a statement regarding the use of every available resource being used to apprehend not only Freedom Walker, but her two sisters, Angel Walker and Destiny Walker. Angel Walker, is wanted for breaking out of jail in Tennessee. Where she was being held under suspicion for twenty plus counts of murder involving a night club shooting.

"Destiny Walker, is wanted for her involvement in the killing of four decorated police officers in, Chicago. F.B.I Director Ennius, has issued a strict warning to the public, not to go near, or try to apprehend *any* of these women. As they're obviously willing to kill, without remorse. If you have any information about the whereabouts of any of these women, you're encouraged to contact your local authorities, or the F.B.I at the number now showing at the bottom of your screen. Eyewitness news is back in sixty seconds."

Despite my desire to shatter the T.V., and the pretty smiling bitch on it. I simply turned it off and tossed the remote on the bed. There was no one I could be mad at besides myself. I'd broken rule number one, by making an emotional decision, over an intelligent one. Truthfully, I'd made *a lot* of emotional decisions as of late. Even though, I was doing all of this in the name of my father. I knew he'd be disappointed.

From the moment he died in my arms, I'd made one bad move after another, and it was time to stop doing that. Hopefully, it wasn't too late. Given the national coverage and spotlight I had shinning on my family. I knew it was my responsibility to get us out of this mess. I couldn't have the blood of anyone I loved on my hands, not again. The sudden vibration of my phone, had me reaching for my pocket, but it wasn't a call or text coming through. It was the alarm for the motion detectors going off. The houses security system was linked directly to my phone, which allowed me to pull up all the camera angles, and what I saw made me smile for the first time in a long time.

Taking a deep breath, I got up from the bed, and made my way downstairs to the front door. To wait on the three-car caravan coming up the two-mile long driveway. One thing I loved about this house I was borrowing, was the fact that it sat way back in the mountains twenty miles from any neighbor, or civilization. The very definition of privacy and it was worth the favor I'd called in for it.

I'd thought my father's black book would provide me with anything for however long I needed. But, with all of our faces plastered on the news, I was hesitant from fear that someone would get spooked. I couldn't go to jail, or die before this was finished, I owed my father.

"Bitch, if you *ever* pull some shit like this on us again. I swear to God, I'll kill you myself," Angel said, as soon as her feet hit the gravel driveway out front.

"I second that motion," Destiny chimed in.

I didn't know how much I missed and needed them, until this very moment, and whatever words I had, got stuck in my throat. So, I just opened my arms wide. Even before they got to me, I could feel the tears sliding down my face. Once we were all huddled together, the sob in my throat tore free, and I finally broke down. Never had there been a time I could remember, where I couldn't control my emotions. Right now, I didn't care, I just needed the unconditional love only these two could give.

"I'm s-sorry," I sobbed.

"Shut up!" Destiny said, squeezing me tighter.

I don't know how long we stayed there crying. But, when I finally pulled back, I could see Black Sam, Big Baby, and Lil' Boy standing right behind my sisters, with tears rolling from their eyes, too.

"Come here you big, softies," I said, smiling through my tears.

"What about me?" asked King Deuce

In all the commotion, I hadn't even noticed King Deuce, and I was more surprised to see him than anyone else.

"Where the fuck did *you* come from?" I asked, pulling him into the ever-growing circle of hugs.

"Come on now, you didn't think I'd let you have *all* the fun by yourself, did you?" He replied, smiling that panty dropping smile of his.

"K.D., this ain't like those other times, this-"

"Save your breath, if I couldn't leave the nigga in Tennessee, then you can bet he's in Seattle as long as we are," Angel said.

"And why *are* we in Seattle?" Destiny asked.

"It's a long story, so let's go inside. I owe you all some answers," I admitted, turning around, leading the way back into the house.

I really hadn't planned on how to say all that needed to be said, but I knew the time had come for the whole truth to be exposed.

"Wow, this is one big ass cabin," Angel said, looking around at the high vaulted ceilings and walls, that boasted stuffed animal heads.

"Yeah, it belongs to a lawyer friend. One I don't have to kill or threaten to get cooperation. There's five bedrooms, three upstairs, and two downstairs. Which means, some people will have to sleep out here in the living room. K.D., I'm assuming the third truck is full of your homies?" I asked, once he'd joined us in the living room.

"Like visa, I never leave home without them."

"That actually might be a good thing this time. *If* you're still here once I've updated everyone," I said honestly.

He didn't say anything, but when he took a seat next to Angel, I saw how he put his arm around her. He tried to make it look casual, but it didn't escape Lil' Boy's notice either, which made me wonder what the fuck was really going on.

"A'ight, Free, now that you've made us public enemy number one. Please explain, why we're not once again fleeing the country right the fuck now," Destiny said.

There was no easy way to say what I needed to, except to hit them with it between the eyes.

"Dad died in my arms, before he did he told me, it was Sapphire who'd shot him. He also told me that Sapphire's son, was his son, our little brother. I don't know how he knew, but he was positive, and the last thing he asked, was that I save him from that bitch. So, my mission has been to find her, so I can get him, and kill her ass once and for all"

I'd expected questions after the conclusion of my speech, but all I was getting from Destiny and Angel, were blank stares. That almost had me worried, until I saw K.D., whisper something in Angel's ear, making her blush and smile in a way, I'd never seen.

"We're *not* having that convo now," Angel said quickly, before turning her attention back to me.

"S-we have a brother?" Destiny asked slowly.

"It would appear that way," I replied.

"And this is the reason you left us, high and dry, no communication, no nothing for the last six months?" Angel asked.

All flirtation was gone from her face now, the anger I'd expected was quickly surfacing.

"A'ight, everybody get out, so I can talk to my sisters," I said, knowing a good fight was coming.

Black Sam, Big Baby, and Lil' Boy moved immediately, heading back towards the front door, but K.D., just sat there looking at Angel.

"My nigga, you ain't hear me?" I asked, irritation clear in my voice.

He still ignored me and didn't move until, Angel, tapped him on the leg. That was definitely something I was gonna address later, but for now, I owed my sisters their say.

"Okay, say whatever you gotta say," I said.

They both looked at each other, but it was Angel who stood up first, and came towards me.

"I only got one thing to say, so listen closely," she said.

I was fully prepared for a vicious tongue lashing. I knew I deserved nothing less for the way I'd acted. What I *wasn't* prepared for was, the swift left jab she fired, that landed squarely in my mouth, but luckily my reflexes kicked in, so her follow-up right hook went wide.

"Bitch, are you crazy?" I yelled, squaring up with her in preparation of getting on her helmet.

"Yep, I'ma show you *just* how crazy," she replied, advancing on me.

Before she could swing again, Destiny, grabbed ahold of her, and slung her down on the couch.

"Sit your silly ass down before you get hurt, and Free, if you make a move towards her, we're *both* gonna whoop your ass, because it's what you deserve," Destiny said, glaring at me in a way that let me know she meant it.

Despite my anger, I used good judgement, because fighting with each other was counterproductive at this point.

"I'm sorry for abandoning you two, leaving you to deal with losing dad on your own. I just didn't – I didn't know how to face you after what happen, because it's my fault he died and I-"

"It's *not* your fault, and you know we never blamed you, not once," Destiny said sincerely.

"I blame myself, though," I admitted, hating the lump of tears, I felt forming in my throat.

"Free, you've been mom and dad to us our whole life. I mean, yes dad was present as much as he could be, and we always knew how much he loved us. But to make us lose you too, that almost broke me," Destiny admitted softly.

Hearing that broke the dam once again, I didn't even try to fight the tears. I hadn't looked at it from their point of view. I'd just been so focused on revenge, I'd almost destroyed everything that mattered.

"I'm s-so sorry, Angel. I love you, I'm sorry," I cried.

This time when she advanced, it wasn't with aggression, instead to she pulled me to her and hug me tightly. Somehow, we all ended up in another group hugging and crying session, when it was over I felt closer to them then I had in forever.

"Nice jab by the way," I said once we'd separated.

"Yeah, something about good dick makes you stronger," Angel, replied nonchalantly.

"What?" Destiny and I, exclaimed in unison.

"I'll explain later, right now we need to know why you've got us out here, and why you did that reckless shit in D.C."

It was hard to move past the fact that my sainted virgin sister, was no longer a virgin. Especially since I knew the dick in question had to be, one of two currently outside. They deserved complete honesty though.

"The move in D.C. had to be made, it was the only way to find out where Sapphire, A.K.A Jewel Sky, is hiding. I admit I didn't think it all the way through, but who the fuck has cameras *inside* their house?"

"Okay, so did you find her, because we saw where you had him doing something on his phone," Destiny said.

"You saw, how would you see – never mind. I almost forgot how good Black Sam, is. Yeah, I found out where she's hiding, but of course the F.B.I would know that I knew by now," I replied.

"And that means she's probably moved again," Angel concluded, shaking her head in frustration.

"Maybe, they were hiding her in New York, and I'm guessing that's because of the volume of people there, so they might feel like they can protect her from us."

"Okay, so why are we literally across the country in Seattle, Washington exactly?" Destiny asked.

"Because our dear deranged mother, with the help of her buddies at the F.B.I, wanted to provide our brother with a good education. Apparently, Seattle has a few good private schools, one of which is home year around to now eleven-year-old Royal Sky," I said.

"She named her son, Royal Sky? No wonder white folks think we come up with some ignorant ass names," Destiny said, shaking her head sadly.

"So, what's the plan?" Angel asked.

"It's simple, we're going to get him, and that will bring her to us. She doesn't know that *we* know about our half-brother, and I verified this. I know, he's still at the school as we speak and security ain't been beefed up."

"You really think she'll come?" Destiny asked.

"I do, it seems the only thing she loves is that little boy," I admitted, feeling my hatred for her grow, with each passing minute.

"If that's the case, it's only fair we take what she loves. Just like she did us."

Chapter 13
Angel

"Bae, I can't even lie, that blonde look adds some more sexy to you, and I didn't think that was possible."

"K.D., just because we're fucking now, don't mean you gotta gas me up," I said, laughing at the fake wounded look on his face.

"You know me better than that, you know you too bad, for me to have to lie about your sexy. In case you don't believe me, though. Here's all the proof you need," he said, pulling his very hard dick out before I could object.

"Boy, what's wrong with you, put that mufucka away!" I demanded, embarrassed that he would do that in the backseat, with two of his niggas in front, and no privacy partition separating us."

"Well, don't insinuate, I'm lying when I give you a compliment. I've only seen you in your natural beauty, besides that one time, but that wig makes me think you might be down for some role playing."

I opened my mouth to call him a liar again, because I rocked different color wigs all the time when I used to dance. But then I remembered, he refused to come in the club, when he knew I was on stage. The one time he did, was when I shot up the club, which wasn't a sexy moment.

"I believe you, you think I'm sexy, but now ain't the time for none of that shit, so please focus," I said, catching sight of the front gate to the private school in the distance.

The Rynburg School for boys, was supposed to be some type of Junior Ivy League that prepared you from elementary school, through high school. Their website said that ninety percent of all students graduated, went on to prestigious schools around the country and abroad. Which explains why one-year tuition started out at eighty thousand per student. If your kid went to this school that meant you had the type of money that don't fold. Or in my brother's, case your mother was a traitorous snitch working for the feds.

From what we'd seen online the place wasn't guarded like a lot of relocated witnesses' kids went here, which probably meant Royal was just special in this situation. Hopefully it wouldn't be hard getting him out of this situation.

"So, what's the play once we get in here?" K.D. asked.

"Well, it's obvious that anyone who has kids here has big money, which means us moving with your homies as security shouldn't look weird. Once we're actually inside, though we're pretty much playing it by ear. Mr. and Mrs. Allen, that would be us, had requested a tour of the grounds, and hopefully we run into my brother. If not then we go looking and shoot our way out if necessary," I replied truthfully.

To this statement, he pulled a chrome Taurus .357 revolver form his inside suit pocket and checked to make sure it was loaded. I already knew my PPQ M2 9mm was ready to rock in my purse. I was really hoping it wouldn't come to that.

"You ready?" He asked once the truck came to a stop.

"Let's do it," I said, putting my big sunglasses on, opening the door to step out.

All of us looked the part with K.D., and his homies wearing matching black suits, and me in a tan form fitting dress with red fuck me pumps. At first, I thought my outfit might be too much, but both Free and Destiny, told me it was just the right amount of sexy to fit the trophy wife stigma. I had to trust their judgement because right now, I was fighting nerves over what we were actually about to do. Killing was one thing, but we were about to kidnap a kid, who has *no idea* of all the skeletons in his family's closet.

"Just breathe, bae," K.D. said, coming up beside me, taking my hand in his.

I felt the reassurance in his grip, that allowed me to put one foot in front of the other as we made our way up the stone steps, through the giant archway. K.D.'s men proceeded us like any security detail would, they had strict instructions to look for any, and all threats.

"Ah, Mr. and Mrs. Allen I presume," said a short, gray-haired white man with a slight British accent.

"And you must be headmaster Worthington, please to meet you, sir," K.D. replied, shaking the man's hand, as if it were the most natural thing in the world.

I was thankful for the oversized sunglasses, because there was no other way to keep a straight face while K.D. put on this show.

"Charmed," I said, offering my hand to be air-kissed by this man, who thought I perceived him as someone beneath my station in life.

"It's my pleasure to make both of your acquaintances. I thank you for coming to tour our prestigious establishment on such short notice. I'm terribly sorry to inform you that we've had a bit of a hiccup that will delay the actual touring of the grounds at this time, but I assure you-"

"Mr. Worthington as I'm sure you can understand my husband and I are very busy people, as such we have to leave the country in the morning. Is there really no way to get a quick peek at all Rynburg has to offer our son?" I asked, trying to ignore the feeling in my stomach that was telling me something was wrong.

"Of course, Mrs. Allen, I was only implying that we would start with the more boring aspect of your introduction to this fine school, by starting with the necessary question, and answer portion in my office. If you would please follow me this way," he requested, turning and leading the way.

It wasn't until then, that I loosened the death grip I had on K.D.'s hand, but I dared not let it go completely. We all followed the little man down the quiet hallway, into an office that looked like every principal's office in any major public school with one exception. There were no kids.

"Mr. Worthington, I can appreciate a quiet learning environment, but where exactly are the children?" I asked.

"Ah, well, that was the hiccup I mentioned earlier. Classes have been dismissed for the day, we're having special visitors from the East Coast. Really just someone coming to get their son do to a family emergency. When that type of thing happens, we try to stop everything so as not to cause a distraction, but no worries because the children always take their studies back to their living quarters."

Hearing this explanation, ratcheted that feeling in my stomach up a notch, and the fact that K.D.'s palms were sweating, meant he was feeling some type of way too. It was starting to look like the statement I made earlier about playing it by ear was about to come into effect.

"So, do things like this happen often?" I asked, nonchalantly.

"Not at all, but as I'm sure you understand from time to time life happens and we must adapt. This particular situation is actually a special case, but I assure you things like this pose very little threat inside."

"I got a bad feeling," I whispered to K.D.

His response was to nod his head and motion for his men to post up outside the door as he closed us inside.

"Let me ask you a question Mr. Worthington, and please be absolutely honest with me. The child who is awaiting the arrival of his family, that would be Royal Sky, right?" K.D. asked.

"I-I'm sorry, who?" Mr. Worthington replied.

It wasn't the shakiness in his voice that gave him away, it was the sudden fear that slid into his pale blue eyes.

"Get him down here *now,*" I ordered, pulling the pistol from my purse, pointing it at him.

"I-."

"Listen fool, you don't wanna fuck with her, or me so, I'm only gonna tell you *one* fucking time to get that boy down here," K.D. warned, pulling his own gun out.

It quickly became clear that Worthington, must be as smart as his students, because he grabbed the phone on his desk, and made the call without further delay.

"How long before his mother gets here?" I asked, lowering my gun long enough to grab my phone from my purse.

"I-I-I don't know, I was just told to expect her and her escorts sometime today."

That meant they could be out front right now for all we know. Quickly, I dialed Free's number, because we were literally about to run for our lives.

"It's me, Sapphire is headed this way, which means we're coming in hot, so everybody needs to be on the move *now,*" I said.

All I got was a one-word response before she disconnected, but I didn't need more because we knew the rendezvous point.

"Do we kill him?" K.D. asked, nodding towards the now trembling man before us.

I gave just enough of a pause to loosen his bowels a little before I spoke.

"Kill him? Nah, I want him to pass on a message. You can do that for me, can't you Mr. Worthington?"

"Yes, yes, of course, whatever you need," he replied quickly.

"Good, now when Jewel Sky arrives, I want you to say these exact words, Father God sends his love. Can you remember that?"

"Y-yes, Father God sends his love," he repeated, shaking his head faster than a bobble head doll.

A knock on the door commanded all of our attention. I motioned for K.D. to follow my lead, and tuck his gun out of sight, so he wouldn't scare Royal. I'd thought I'd been prepared to see my little brother for the first time. However, nothing could've prepared me for the boy who walked through that door. He was a mirror image of Father God, an undeniable clone if I'd ever seen one, and I felt my knees threaten to give out.

"Who are you?" He asked K.D., sizing him up with eyes full of distrust.

"Your mom sent us," I said, stepping in front of K.D., to put focus on myself.

"My mom sent you. Is that true Mr. Worthington?" He asked, looking past me to his headmaster.

"It is, young Royal," he replied, in a surprisingly calm voice.

For a minute, no one spoke and Royal simply continued to evaluate me, and K.D. in a surprisingly thorough manner for his young age. The same way our father would have.

"You look familiar," he said to me.

The way he made that statement inspired me to extend my hand for him to take, and thankfully he did.

"Don't forget that message," I called over my shoulder, as I led my little brother from the office, and out into the hallway.

K.D. and his men were right behind us, and we headed for the front door at a swift pace, but not so fast as to alarm Royal. I'd halfway expected to come face to face with the F.B.I out front, but it seemed like our luck would hold a little longer.

"Are we going to New York?" Royal asked once we were in the truck.

"No, we're going to L.A. right now, then somewhere else, but that's a surprise," I replied, truthfully.

"I don't like surprises and please don't bullshit or patronize me like I'm a little kid."

At first his statement fucked me up, but I quickly realized that it shouldn't have because this boy was a Walker, no matter who'd raised him.

"Fair enough. We're going to a family reunion," I said.

"I don't have any family, it's just me, and my mom so-."

"You *do* have family. The reason I look so familiar to you, is because I'm your sister," I told him, taking my glasses off so he could see my entire face.

Whatever he was thinking, he kept closely guarded because his face remained blank.

"My s-sister? So, then you know who my dad is?"

"I do. The question is do *you* know who he is?" I asked.

The slow shaking of his head made my heart hurt, because I knew the truth of all this was too much for a kid his age, but it was what he deserved. Only time would tell if he was Walker tough.

Aryanna

Chapter 14
Destiny

"This is some bullshit!"

"Baby listen, I-."

"No Destiny, don't give me that baby listen shit, like I'm not understanding or comprehending. You *need* me goddammit!" She yelled, becoming angrier by the second. In the back of my mind I'd known this fight was coming. But, knowing that still didn't give me a way to prepare for it, or a solution of how to win it. All I knew was right now I didn't have *time* for it.

"Samantha, you're right I do need you. I need the skills only you possess. I need the unconditional love, only you can give me. What I need most right now, is for you to stop refusing because you're getting on the goddamn plane no matter *what* you say! In Brazil you said you wanted the old me back, that's who I am right now. So, you gotta understand that I can't do what needs to be done if I'm worried about you. The *whole world* is looking for us right now, instead of running, we're getting ready to bring the fight to their front door. I need to be completely focus for that," I said, softening my tone slightly, because the tears she'd been fighting we're now cascading down her beautiful face.

Sending her away wasn't done to cause pain, it actually was strategic in the grand scheme of things. It was just hard for her to see that right now because, she was scared of losing me, and we both knew, I couldn't offer any hollow assurances about how that wouldn't happen. The reality was that me and my sisters probably would die, but that was something we were willing to face in order to see this thing through. One thing we were all sure of was, that we damn sure wouldn't be the only ones to die.

"We're here, and that's K.D.'s truck right there next to the plane," Lil' Boy said from the front passenger seat.

I didn't know how the fuck they'd gotten down here before we did, but it was a blessing, because I wouldn't feel anything like safety until we were thirty thousand feet up. Even then, I knew it would only be temporary. Big Baby and Lil' Boy got out, but when Black Sam, went to do the same I grabbed her arm to keep her where she was.

"Please tell me you understand," I said softly, scooting closer to her.

"You know I understand, but that don't mean I gotta like it, and it damn sure don't mean, I gotta accept losing you."

"I'd never ask you to accept that, because that's not something *I'm* prepared to accept. You know this is what has to happen though, and God forbid something does happen to me. I want you to be the one who keeps everyone else we love safe. Can you do that for me, bae?" I asked, taking her face in my hands, looking directly into her eyes.

The pain I saw in them, hurt me beyond words, but the strength I saw behind that pain added to my own strength. The kiss I placed on her lips was soft, sensual, almost innocent in its purity, and in that way, it was exactly like our love for one another, so it was fitting. A tap on the rear window interrupted us and I could see Free, standing outside the door, which meant it was time.

Come on," I said, taking her hand, pulling her across the seat so she could follow me out of the truck.

"We gotta move, the amber alert has already been issued," Free, said as soon as my feet hit the asphalt.

We'd anticipated this of course, but we'd hoped to be at our second stop before that type of shit hit the fan. Grabbing, our stuff from the back of the truck, we hurried to board the G I.V. jet, Free, had somehow managed to get for our travels. My intentions were to take Samantha into the back bedroom and have a slightly different conversation during our flight, but as soon as I saw the little boy sitting on the leather sofa all coherent thoughts left my mind.

"Da-damn," I mumbled, trying to cover the fact that I almost called him daddy.

"Spooky ain't it," Angel said, from her seat next to him.

One look in Free's direction, and I could tell she was as fucked up as I was.

"Uh, why are they looking at me like that?" Royal asked.

The look on Angels' face said she didn't wanna answer that question, but she knew she had to.

"Apparently, Royal, saw dad once because he'd been Face Timing with his mom, when a commotion broke out in her hotel room, and she'd turned her tablet until they came face to face. And then the signal was lost," Angel replied.

I had no doubt that Free was putting the pieces together with the same speed that I was, and now we knew how Sapphire had gotten the drop on them.

"Why do you keep calling her *my* mom, I thought we all had the same mother *and* father?" Royal asked, looking first at Angel and then in our direction.

I could see the war of emotions written all over Free's face, and since I had no idea which was about to win I decided to step in.

"We do have the same mom and dad, it's just different for us because we weren't raised by her," I said, sitting next to him.

"Oh, well did you all have to move around a lot too?" He asked, again looking at Angel, for his answer.

"Babe, I want you to go set up in the back and we'll be there in a minute," I said, thankful to feel the plane beginning to taxi onto the runway.

Black Sam, did like I asked and Angel continued to answer Royal's questions, which gave me a minute to talk to Free.

"You okay?" I whispered, once I'd pulled her out of earshot of everyone else.

"Sh-she used that boy to kill his father, *our father,*" she replied, her voice shaking as much as her body was at the moment.

I knew all too well the blind rage that Free, was getting ready to go into, and I couldn't let that happen, not now at least.

"Freedom, look at me, we'll get her. I promise, but right now you gotta keep the leash on that animal, we gotta keep our little brother calm. We don't know how he's gonna react if he thinks somethings wrong, so the best thing to do is *remain calm,*" I said, putting both of my hands on her shoulders, forcing her to look me in the eye.

The battle inside her was *real,* but thankfully, I saw the moment she put all the emotion away and returned to thinking logically.

"That's my girl, now please go to the back of the plane because we need to have a strategy meeting," I requested.

Just then the seatbelt light came on, so we were all forced to grab a seat, and wait for takeoff. It was a full ten minutes before I took a deep breath, but I knew it was only temporary because we had to land on U.S. soil one more time.

"Angel," I said, getting her attention, nodding towards the rear cabin so she would move in that direction.

"Listen, I need to go talk with our sisters for a minute, but you're okay with the guys here, right?" Angel asked.

In response to her question Royal looked from K.D. to Lil' Boy, to Big Baby, and back to K.D.

"You got a phone with games on it?" He asked K.D.

"I think we can work something out," K.D. replied, smiling, and moving to occupy the seat Angel, was vacating.

I could tell that Big Baby and Lil' Boy didn't feel slighted, and knowing them the way I did, I knew they weren't exactly kid friendly anyways. The smile Angel gave K.D., didn't escape my attention either, nor did the scowl it caused to appear on Lil' Boy's face.

"Okay, before we get to the business, bitch you got some explaining to do," I said, pointing at Angel, once we were closed in the rear cabin.

"What you talking 'bout?" She asked, trying to feign innocence.

"Now see, your whole innocent look has worked for you because it was true. But, I *know* you done gave up the cookies, and my money is on Vontae," I said.

"Noooo!" Black Sam said once again, this time taking her attention completely away from the laptop in front of her, so she wouldn't miss any more tea being spilt.

"Damn y'all all *in* my business," Angel said, laughing.

If she thought that comment was gonna take her ass off the hot seat, she had really lost her damn mind. No one said a word, we just sat there looking at her, blinking real slow.

"Ugh, y'all make me sick! Okay, fine, yes, I had sex with Vontae and-"

"Was it good?" Black Sam, asked.

"Did you use protection?" Free asked, seriously.

"Yes and yes, damn. Any more questions?"

"You know Lil' Boy gonna kill that nigga, right?" I asked, watching her closely to see if that possibility had even crossed her mind.

Her mouth hanging wide open and no words moving past her lips told me, she hadn't thought of it before, but it was *definitely* on her satellite now.

"Rule number one, there's nothing more powerful in the world than pussy, not even money. It'll make a nigga act a goddamn fool, especially if its good," Free preached.

"Well she's just starting, so it'll take time before she got that whip appeal," Black Sam said.

"Bitch please, that nigga ain't last ten minutes, and you know his reputation," Angel replied laughing cockily.

"Yeah, you *definitely* gonna get that nigga killed because his nose is open now for sure," I said, shaking my head.

"That's tomorrows problem, lets focus on today's," Free said, in a serious tone signaling play time being over.

"Right, so, when do you want me to release the hotel footage?" Black Sam asked.

"Pull it up and let me look at it," Free replied.

I don't understand why she insisted on continuously doing that, when we all knew the images wouldn't change, and the knowledge they carried would still hurt just as much. There hadn't been any cameras in Sapphire's room that night, but Black Sam had been covering every angle in that hallway. What we'd seen that the general public wasn't privy to was Sapphire, exit the hotel room with the gun she'd used to kill our father still in her hands, and the F.B.I helping her get away.

This all happened moments before Free, had arrived on the scene. Only we knew this footage existed because Black Sam, had to wipe the hotels server, so they wouldn't see our father killing the F.B.I. At this point, though it didn't matter and since the manhunt was on for us. We intended to bring some scrutiny towards the beloved Federal Bureau of Investigation.

"You got everything we need out of that file too?" Free asked, after watching the video.

"Yeah and it's a good thing too, because when I hacked back in to triple check it was *completely* gone. You know I'm good at what I do, but whoever they had do that was a fucking magician," Sam said, shaking her head.

None of us was surprised that they were trying to cover their trail, the government had been good at conspiracies long before we were born.

"Okay, I'll call you, and tell you when to send everything to all the major news outlets."

"Free, are you sure your plan is gonna work? I mean do you really wanna do it this way?" I asked, cautiously.

She knew I wasn't second guessing our decision to go public, or the all-out war we intended to wage from that point on. I was asking about the personal decision she was gonna have to make with regards to my nephew and his father.

"There's no other way. We'll be in Atlanta in five hours, it's time to face the music."

Aryanna

Chapter 15
Freedom

A mission gives me focus, but this one in particular had me feeling like a shark that smells blood in the water, because there was hunger accompanying that focus. I *needed* this, I needed to kill that nothing ass bitch, even if it meant I had to give my life to do it. Death wasn't what I feared. What had my heart racing and my chest tight, was on the other side of the back door I was standing in front of, but I'd come too far to turn back now. With a quick look around, I took a deep breath, and tapped twice on the steel door. The slide in the door revealed eyes I was all too familiar with and without hesitation the door opened bringing me face to face with my baby daddy. Even with only inches separating us, it was still clear that we were worlds apart, and I knew that was my fault.

I opened my mouth to speak, but I would've been doing it to his back because he'd already turned and headed back into the house. I followed his lead, trying to ignore how his behavior stung, making sure to lock and bolt the door behind me. Once upon a time, this had just been a money house because neither of us believed in banks, but as I followed Bone, past the kitchen and into the living room I noticed he'd turned it into primary residence. He had everything from baby bottles, to a big screen in this mufucka. Seeing the bottles made me feel even more guilt, I'd always envisioned myself breastfeeding when I finally became a mother. I halfway expected to see my son when I walked in the living room, but I was spared the agony, and guilt of having to face him right now.

"Where's our-"

"*My* son is sleeping upstairs, so whatever you came here to say I'd appreciate if you kept your voice down,"

Bone said, turning to face me, crossing his arms over his chest.

By no stretch of the imagination did I think this reunion would be all rainbows and hearts, but the coldness in his tone was something I'd never heard before. As bad as it made me feel, I knew I had no right to feel anything right now.

"I know you probably hate me, and I'm not here to convince you not to. What I did, the way I left, was entirely fucked up, and both of you deserved better than that. You deserve better than me because right now, I'm on a path of destruction that's gonna take everybody around me straight to hell. The most important thing I need you to understand. Is that I love you both, as much as I've ever loved anything, or anyone in this world or beyond. I know I can't be the mother B.J. needs, but I know you'll be *everything* he needs because you're-"

"Don't," he said forcefully.

"Don't what?" I asked, confused.

"Don't you fucking stand there and say goodbye to me like I'm gonna accept it. I *don't* accept it, you hear me? I don't – fucking – accept it," he growled through clenched teeth, advancing on me quicker than any lion stalking a gazelle.

Before I knew it, his hand was around my throat, and he'd backed me into the living room wall with such force, it forced the air from my lungs. My first thought was that this nigga done lost his *entire* mind, but the look in his eyes stopped me from reaching for my gun or fighting back in anyway. The anger was there, but it was superficial. The pain was real, I knew that the moment the first tear won the battle of wills and slid down his face. In all the years I'd known him I'd never seen him cry, not once, but seeing it now put shit into perspective for me real quick.

What he did next surprised me, as much as his tears did. Using the hand still gripping my neck, he lifted me off my feet, bringing me eye level to him. At the same time his lips descended on mine in a feverish hunger. From the moment our tongues touched, I felt like I was drowning. I welcomed it, locking both my arms and legs around him tightly. Suddenly, his hand went from my throat to my ass, the firmness of his grip had my pussy singing like Trey Songz.

We stayed locked like that, blindly stumbling down the hallway, and bouncing off of walls until we came to the one bedroom that was on this floor. The bed was a twin, but neither of us gave a damn. He tossed me on it like a rag doll. I was too busy worrying about getting naked to care and he was following my lead. I'd heard somewhere that we were supposed to wait six weeks after the baby to have sex, but right now I wanted his big black dick in every hole on my body.

If three weeks is too soon, oh well!

"Oh fuck!" I moaned, once he'd pounded me with his first stroke.

Three blows later and I felt my pussy open like a beautiful flower and rain all over him, and that seemed to push him to the brink of insanity. Before I could agree or disagree he had me on my back bent in half, feeding me long, toe curling strokes, that would make any bitch beg.

"Bone-Bone-Bone!" I chanted, wanting to fuck him back, but helpless, and quickly becoming a slave to the dick.

He knew it too because somehow, he was diving deeper, making me think the dick would push my stomach through my mouth. I *loved* it! Within minutes I was coming again, but before my knees could stop shaking, he flipped me over roughly, and dove back inside me. Our love making quickly took on all the sounds of a real live fist fight, but at least on my hands, and knees I could throw that ass back at him. The way he growled made my entire body tingle. I knew I almost had him or at least I thought I did.

Trying to get cute cost me, before I knew it he'd knocked my knees from under me, putting me flat on my stomach, and without warning he was balls deep in my asshole.

"Baby-wait-I-."

"Shut up!" He barked, plowing steadily into me. I couldn't deny how good it felt, and if I thought my climax would have to rebuild he was proving me wrong.

"Ohhh-oh shit, Bone I'mmmm--"

The rest of the sentence was lost in a scream as I felt his hot cum shoot into my ass, and that got me off quicker than a starters pistol. The orgasm was blinding, literally, leaving my vision filled with white spots. The satisfaction was undeniable though. We stayed stacked like a deck of cards for a few minutes until he reluctantly rolled out of me and laid on the bed facing me. I'd thought our battle would exercise all our demons, but there were still tears in his eyes, and that hurt my heart.

"Baby, I'm sorry," I said, wiping his cheeks and hating myself a little more.

"I don't want you to be sorry Freedom, I want you to be *better*. That little boy upstairs needs you, *I* need you. Don't you get that?"

"I do, it's just-I don't know how to be a mother. I don't know how to let this go, especially now that it's so close to finally being over."

"Over? Is that what you really think? When did you become so naïve? The Free, I know would understand that this doesn't end until we're *all* in boxes. Is that what you want for our son?" He asked.

There was no anger in his words, but that made the truth of what he said ring louder to me. I did understand that death could be around the corner, but not for him.

"You're not getting in this fight Bone."

"I damn well--"

"Baby I didn't come back here to argue with you. I came to reason with you and explain what has to happen next so just listen. We've got a plan, the F.B.I has us all over the news like the spawn of Adolf Hitler. But, they've got their own secrets they don't want exposed. We've got video of my mother walking out of that hotel room, gun in hand, with F.B.I escorts. Then we have a copy of the file that proves they framed my father all those years ago."

"Okay, what do you plan to do with that info?" He asked, his curiosity piqued.

"We release it to every major news outlet and try them in the court of public opinions just like they're doing us. We change the narrative."

"A'ight, so the F.B.I has egg on their face, but how does that solve the ultimate goal of Sapphire?"

"We're gonna bring her to us because we have the one thing she loves most," I replied smiling.

"You have the-oh God, tell me that Amber Alert on the West Coast earlier today wasn't you mufuckas."

"It is, but I can explain because there's some things I haven't told you. Before my father died he told me about Sapphire's son, and that he believed the little boy was his. He asked me to get him and protect him, and that's exactly what I'ma do," I stated firmly.

"Yeah, and use him as bait, huh?"

"Not exactly, he'll be with Black Sam, Big Baby, and Lil' Boy in Brazil until this is over, along with you, and B.J.," I added, softly.

The curiosity in his eyes vanished and anger was back quicker than lightening, but he didn't say shit, he just got up.

"Bone?"

"You must be out your rabid ass mind for real, if you think I'ma let you invite the devil to your door, and *I'm* not here to help. I know you hit your head a few times while we were fucking, but I didn't think I gave you a concussion," he said, pulling his shorts, and t-shirt back on.

"Stop cracking jokes because I'm serious and--"

"Nah, *you* the one with jokes, and if that's what you wanna talk about then this conversation is over," he said, walking out of the room, slamming the door.

I'd known coming into this, this mufucka was more stubborn than any jackass ever made. Still, I'd thought he'd see reason because of our son. He was leaving me no choice, except to do some ugly shit. Getting up sent aftershocks through my body from what had just happened to it, but I damn sure had no regrets. I quickly pulled on my own shorts and t-shirt, pulled my phone out, and moved as far away from the closed door as I could.

"How'd it go?" Angel asked, answering on the first ring.

"Better than I expected, but he's not even trying to hear me on him taking B.J. and leaving."

"Told you that, so what's your play?" She asked.

"Your already know. How's Royal doing?"

"Sound asleep, Black Sam, is watching over him waiting on the word from you."

A quick look at my phone screen showed the time as almost midnight. The plan was to have everyone who needed to be on the plane in the air by sunrise.

"Okay, tell Sam to open the floodgates at 2 a.m. so every station has breaking overnight news by 6 a.m. The lawyer assured me that once the heat is on he'll be able to get to Sapphire, without the F.B.I.'s interference. They'll be trying to distance themselves a little. She'll get the message to come on home and when she does you know what's next."

"Are you sure you wanna do this to Bone?" She asked.

"No, I don't want to, but I have to, so just be here by 5 a.m.," I replied, disconnecting the call before she could talk me out of it.

Taking a deep breath, I put my phone away, picked up my gun off the floor where I'd slung it, and checked to see if the safety was on. In the name of love, I'd do anything for my family, anything.

Aryanna

Chapter 16
Angel

"I take it Free's talk with Bone went how we expected?" Destiny asked, as soon as my call was over.

"Pretty much, and if we know our sister she used every bit of persuasion she had in her," I replied.

"I don't blame him," Lil' Boy commented.

"What?" Destiny asked.

"I said I don't blame him. I mean what nigga is really gonna leave the woman he loves to fight and possibly die? While he's off on some beach sipping something fruity, that's weak shit."

At the moment, we were all sitting around the living room in the house that Big Baby and Lil' Boy shared, while Royal was upstairs sleeping. Hearing Lil' Boy's statement brought Destiny's eyes straight to mine, and we both knew what he'd said wasn't only about Free and Bone. Ever since Destiny, had asked me if I knew, Lil' Boy was gonna kill K.D. I'd been watching him closer, and I was definitely picking up on a vibe that we didn't need right now. K.D. wasn't stupid either because he never let him out of his sight or put himself in a situation that was a physical disadvantage to Lil' Boy. I was already in the middle of one war. I didn't need was the jealousy I detected in Vermont to spill over now.

"Free, wants you to start leaking info at 2 a.m., so you should go ahead and start preparing for that Black Sam. Lil' Boy let me holla at you in the back for a second," I said, getting up from my seat next to K.D. on the couch.

I felt K.D. try to grab my hand, but I shook him off, keeping my eyes on Lil' Boy as he slowly rose to his full height. I was thankful K.D. didn't make a grab for me again because the tension in the room felt like dynamite with a lit fuse.

"K.D. go upstairs and check on Royal," I called over my shoulder, hoping to distract him while I straightened this other nigga.

Having been here a few times before I knew the layout of the house, so I led the way knowing Lil' Boy would follow. I didn't put it past K.D. not to eavesdrop though. So, instead of going straight down the hall into the back bedroom. I took my second left and went down into the basement. There was nothing down here except wide open space and enough weapons to make the military think twice before coming in.

"I ain't got time for your bullshit my nigga," I said, as soon as we were downstairs in the furthest corner away from the door.

"My bullshit? What about you?"

"I ain't on bullshit, I'm focused on what the fuck is about to go down and you need-"

"What *I* need is for you to be real with your goddamn self for a minute! Ever since we got back to the states you been taking reckless chances for that pretty nigga upstairs, and for what? Every time you deal with dude shit goes sideways and you end up in a fucked-up situation, and *who's* there to save your ass? Who just spent the last six months freezing his dick off by your side? It damn sure wasn't pretty Ricky upstairs! It was *me*, the nigga who's *always there*, the nigga who'd die for you, the one who truly loves you no matter what! But I'm the one you want to go to Brazil while you let him stand beside you in the trenches, right? Which one of us is on bullshit Angel?"

In all the years I'd known him, he'd *never* blown my shit back like this, never just went *the* fuck off, and spoke his mind. I wasn't oblivious to how he felt or what he meant to me. But, it was obvious I'd made the mistake a lot of women made in taking a good man for granted. I hadn't just ignored his feelings though, I'd ignored my own too. In this moment, I had no choice except to admit that I did love this man in front of me, *and* the one upstairs. The question was what the fuck did I do about it.

"Lil' Boy, I-oh, fuck it," I said, pulling him towards me until he leaned down, and kissed me.

This was in no way what I had planned when I asked him to talk, but I wanted him inside me just as bad as I had K.D.

"Are you sure about this?" he asked, pulling back slightly to look down into my eyes.

I wasn't hearing the question he asked, as much as I was the words he'd spoken to me moments ago, because they were all true. He'd given me his love and loyalty without questions and I knew he'd always be there for me. What more could any woman ask for?

"This is what I want, but you have to understand that things are complicated. I won't lie to you and say I don't have feelings for K.D. because I do, but I love you too, and that's why this ain't wrong. When this is all over we'll figure this shit out, if you want," I replied, leaving it up to him how this went.

"You know that's what I want, but don't think sleeping with me is gonna convince me to leave the country because I told you I'd die for you and I meant-"

"I don't need you to die for me, I *need* ya to live for me," I said, taking his face in my hands. I could tell by the chaos of emotions swimming in his eyes, he understood how important that was to me, and with that I knew our conversation was complete.

"We need to hurry," I said, pulling his lips towards mine again, already craving the taste of him.

Immediately I felt his fingers on the buttons to my shorts and within seconds he had me naked from the waist down. When I went to return the favor, so I could get at that monster I knew he was working with. I was suddenly tossed into the air like a cheerleader at the top of a high school pyramid.

"What are you doing?" I asked, slightly panicked, but thankful for the ceiling beam I was gripping.

"Just hang on," he instructed, putting both of my legs on his shoulders which put him face deep in my pussy.

At that point I had no questions, I was simply fighting not to release the screams clanging at my throat as his tongue introduced itself in a way I'd never known.

"Holy-holy shit!" I whispered, determined to bite a hole in my lip rather than alert everyone upstairs about what was taking place with us.

His licks were slow and thorough like I was his favorite Ice cream I could feel my juices rushing into his mouth like I'd left the water on. The moment his lips closed around my clit I came so hard, I feared I'd pass out, letting go of the ceiling, and gripping his head like koala bear.

"Oh, please, don't-don't-don't!" I begged, but he kept right on eating me until my world moved on its axis again.

He drank from me like I was communion wine at church and he needed saving, only letting me down off his shoulders when his thirst was quenched. I had doubts about my legs holding me up, but I didn't have a chance to find out. Because he only lowered me enough to feel the head of his dick slip in between my throbbing pussy lips. I'd thought I was mentally prepared for what came next, but when he backed me into the nearest wall, and slowly pushed inside me, I knew I had no way to prepare for this.

"It's-it's-too m-much!" I moaned, breathlessly.

"I'll take it slow," he promised, kissing me passionately.

I'd never tasted myself, especially not on another man, and the whole experience of it was intoxicating. True to his word he gave me the slowest, most tender strokes I could've asked for, allowing me to open myself to him until I knew I was ready.

"Now fuck me," I demanded, biting his lip until I tasted blood.

His response was to take me from the wall to the floor, and I was glad it was carpeted because he wasn't playing no games at this point. All dick wasn't the same, and he was proving this with pounding blows that I could feel all the way up in my throat. I wasn't into kinky shit, but I made him put his hand over my mouth because I no longer had a choice on whether to scream.

Suddenly, I heard the door open. "Yo, Angel you down there?" Destiny yelled from the top steps, freezing Lil' Boy in mid-stroke.

"Y-Yea, I'm coming now," I yelled back, in as normal a voice as I could.

Her response was to close the door back, but before the lock clicked Lil' Boy was already moving again with his hand over my mouth. I hadn't lied either because within minutes we both came in strangled moans and growls. The look on his face said he wanted to do anything except stop, but we both understood that our wants had to take a backseat.

"D-did you tell him you love him?" Lil' Boy asked, trying to catch his breath, but still on top, and very much inside me.

"No. Why?"

"Because I know he was your first, I wouldn't disrespect you by assuming otherwise," he replied.

I wasn't quite sure how to respond, but I could see the pure vulnerability all over Lil' Boy's face in this moment. All I had to offer him was the truth though.

"He was my first, but not my first love. This situation is complicated like I said, but I'll never lie to you. I loved you first."

When he leaned down to kiss me it was with a tenderness I'd never knew I wanted until now, and truthfully it fucked me up more than the sex had.

"Come on, we've got work to do," he said, finally pulling out of my sore pussy, helping me to my feet.

Once I had my clothes back on, I looked over us both hoping we appeared completely normal. The last thing I wanted was him and K.D. going at it.

"Please act normal when we go back up there," I said.

"Don't worry I will."

"That big ass grin on your face *ain't* normal," I replied, punching him in the arm.

He laughed, even though he knew I was serious, but then he fixed his face in the same pissed expression he'd been wearing.

"Thanks," I said, giving him a quick kiss before leading the way back upstairs.

"Go find Big Baby and act like you need to talk and send Destiny back to the bedroom, I gotta take a shower," I whispered in his ear, before opening the basement door.

He gave me a shit-eating grin at the shower comment but nodded his head anyway. Thankfully, no one was waiting on us in the hallway, and I made it into the spare bedroom uninterrupted. No sooner had I closed the door. I made a bee line for the bathroom and turned the shower on, knowing I smelled like sex. Not just sex, *great* sex, I couldn't lie because the sex with Vontae had been great too. But, Lil Boy had me wondering why a bitch had *waited* so long! Now here I was getting ready to face death within the next twenty-four hours with nothing but penis on the brain.

"Think bitch and prioritize," I said to myself.

"Who you talking to, and why you running the shower?" Destiny asked from outside the bathroom door. As soon as I turned around to face her, her eyes lit up like a Christmas tree.

"Ooooh, no you *didn't*!"

"You're right, I didn't. Why were you calling me?" I asked, turning my back to her, beginning to undress.

"Bitch you lying!" She exclaimed, stepping into the bathroom, closing the door.

I didn't respond, but I damn sure kept my back to her, so she wouldn't see the smile on my face.

"Oh wow, now I can smell it on you, so that shower is a damn good idea," she said, chuckling.

"Fuck you, don't judge me because it just kinda happened," I replied, stepping beneath the blistering water.

"Hey, you ain't gotta explain shit to me. I've known for years that dick is a beautiful thing. Welcome to the party but remember what I told you on the plane. Lil' Boy will *undoubtedly* kill that nigga K.D. now," she warned, in a serious tone.

Right now, that was the last thing I wanted to think about, so I switched subjects.

"What did you want, Destiny?"

"Oh, Free, called back and said Bone was sleeping like a baby."

"She really hit that nigga over the head with her pistol, then drugged him?" I asked, in disbelief that she really went through with her plan.

"Yep, all in the name of love. Sweet huh?"

"Man, that nigga is gonna be homicidal mad when he wakes up." I replied, washing myself quickly and thoroughly, trying not to be alarmed by the blood on my thighs.

There'd been blood with Vontae too because he'd popped my cherry. I had a feeling this came from Lil Boy having too much dick. If there was such a thing.

"He's gonna wake up on a beach far away, and hopefully we'll be in route, so he'll only be a little mad. We got another problem though."

"What's that, did she give him too much of that horse tranquilizer?" I asked.

"Nah, only a little more than we gave Royal, and he's fine by the way. No, the problem is she doesn't know what to do because B.J. is up and he's crying." I pulled the shower curtain back to see if she was serious, and I didn't find a smile on her face.

"What the hell do *we* know about babies, she's the mama bear of us three," I replied.

"Yeah I know. Truthfully, I think she's scared of her own son, but I don't know why."

"Maybe It's that postpartum shit you hear about, it doesn't just happen to white people, you know?" I said, turning the water off, grabbing a towel off the rack.

"I don't know, maybe, but either way she wants us to come over now and help."

I thought about this request as I quickly put my clothes back on, knowing, it was a big deal for Free to ask for help. At the same time, she'd always taught us to face our fears head on.

"We'll get there at 5:00 a.m. like we planned, we've still got a lot of shit to do," I said.

"Are you gonna be the one to call and tell her?"

"Nope, a text will do just fine," I replied, ignoring the smile on Destiny's face, leading the way out of the bathroom.

As soon as I walked into the living room, I could feel K.D. trying to stare a hole through the side of my skull, but I chose to address business instead of personal.

"Listen up, shit is gonna get crazy in the next few hours, so we need to start getting our shit together. Because we don't know if Sapphire will be able to escape the F.B.I.'s net to arrive in Atlanta alone. We gotta be ready for an all-out shit storm. Big Baby, Lil Boy, that means we'll be picking from the arsenal downstairs, but you've gotta take shit with you, too. According to Destiny there's nothing at the house in Brazil. Stop giving me those looks, you know why you have to go with Black Sam, Bone, and the baby. K.D. what's up with your people?"

"They're on the way as soon as I make the call," he replied.

"Make the call," I ordered.

"Everything is ready to go on my end," Black Sam said.

"Good. If everything goes as planned, this will all be over in the next forty-eight hours."

Aryanna

Chapter 17
Freedom

I'd faced death more times than I could remember, and thus far had managed to come out victorious. I credited not only my survival instincts and skills, but the fact that I didn't fear death, because it was one of life's few guarantees. So, how was it that I was terrified of the little boy sleeping in my arms, right now? During the planning phase of what I possibly had to do to my beloved, Bone. I somehow neglected to factor in that someone had to take care of B.J.

My emergency call to my sisters resulted in a text, that was gonna get *both* their asses kicked whenever they did get here. At first, I'd been willing to let him cry himself back to sleep, while I went through the house packing everything him, and his father would need for the trip, but that little nigga was *pissed*! It became clear really quick, that he had me, and his daddy's temperament. I fixed him a bottle, which of course he couldn't hold by himself, so I was forced to hold him and feed him.

My fear was real, but something happened between feeding him, burping him, and him going back to sleep that changed me. I couldn't put it into words. I'd been sitting in the same rocking chair in the nursery Bone, built watching my little man sleep. I'd never witnessed so much innocence in one person, or such perfection. The fear that I had when it came to taking care of him was gone.

I could feel new fear sliding into its place. What if I wasn't here to take care of him? I had no doubts that Bone, would be a helluva dad, and my sisters and I, were proof a good father could raise a child. But, I didn't want my son to be like us. I wanted him to be a good person, a respectable man, that didn't live his life by bullets, and bodies.

I hadn't questioned my decisions up until this point. Now here I sat in the middle of the night, knowing I owed this little boy a life. Even though, I knew this, and could now admit it to myself. I also knew it was too late to go back. The hour had come and gone for Black Sam, to fire our next shots in the war, and the media was eating it up like it was Watergate. When you had a president that has been under as much scrutiny as Trump.

Anything that sounds like a government conspiracy, will get more attention than a Kardashian pregnancy. I'd counted on that, and it would seem that my bet was paying off. That meant there was no going back now. The sound of someone banging on the door downstairs, interrupted the bonding moment I was having with my son. I knew who it was and that the time had come.

"Come on little guy, time to go meet your crazy ass family," I said, standing with him, making my way downstairs.

"Oh, *now* you bitches show up," I said, stepping to the side, letting everyone move past me.

"You survived didn't you, now, give me my nephew," Angel demanded, gently lifting B.J., from my arms.

Unlike when I was in the hospital, I had a hard time letting him go. I knew I needed to refocus in order to survive for him. While Angel, Destiny, and Black Sam, fussed over my newborn in the living room. I pulled the fellas into the kitchen, so we could get some shit straight.

"Big Baby and Lil' Boy, you know to go *straight* to the airfield from here, right? The plane has already been refueled. Not even the pilot knows where y'all are going. You'll have to tell him once you're on board."

"We got it Free, what do you want us to do about Bone, though?" Lil' Boy asked.

"The dose I hit him with will last for twelve hours. Before it wears off, I want you to give him one more dose. That goes for Royal too, hopefully by the time that wears off we're all headed your way."

"I don't know Free, that nigga might try to kill us before you get there," Lil' Boy replied nervously.

"Nah, you family, but just in case I wouldn't give him a gun if I were you. Why don't you and your brother, load him up while I holla at K.D.? Bone's in the living room on the couch."

As they moved past me to take care of that, I turned my focus on King Deuce, knowing there were two conversations that needed to take place.

"Before I get to the business I'ma address the personal. You know that I know you better than anyone, and I fuck with you. But, if you fuck my sister over, I won't hesitate to cut your balls off, and shove them down your throat," I warned him, smiling sweetly, so he'd understand the enjoyment I'd get from it.

"Okay Don Corleone," he replied in his best Italian accent.

"Take me for a joke if you want my nigga. Believe me when I tell you, all the mufuckas you got behind you, can't save you."

"Look, I get it and I know my reputation. Angel is different though. I mean she's cut from a totally different cloth, than any woman I've known. Trust me I swore off fucking virgins a *long* time ago, because that's a headache I wouldn't wish on anyone. I felt honored to be Angel's first, though. On some real shit, I'm thinking about leaving the country with you all once I've got my business running smoothly and I've tied up all my loose ends," he said, sincerely.

Hearing him say this was a surprise to me, one thing I knew about K.D., was that he was Memphis to the core. He'd rather die in them streets, than live anywhere in the world. Little sis' must have inherited that thunder cat like the rest of us and put it on his ass righteously.

"I know the loose ends, have a lot to do with your mom. I'm sorry about what happened to her. As it pertains to Angel, all I'm gonna say is that the road to hell is paved with good intentions, and you don't wanna go to hell because I'm the devil."

"Your warning is heard loud and clear," he replied.

"Good, now let's get down to business. Is your team in route?"

"I'm expecting them here before sunrise, locked and loaded. All you gotta do is tell me where you want them."

"Once we're sure this bitch is coming, we're gonna secure everything from a mile out to the actually rendezvous point. That way there's no chance of escape," I said, picturing the blood bath in my mind already.

"You know, killing more F.B.I. agents is only gonna make them come at you harder, right?" he asked.

"In for a penny, in for a pound my nigga."

Just then, we were interrupted by his phone going off. He simply looked at the screen instead of answering it.

"Your other bitch?" I asked sarcastically.

"Funny, but no, my team just got in the city limits. I need to go meet them."

"A'ight, but don't bring them here, just wait for my call," I said.

"Got it." He headed for the door, but I saw him glance in the direction of the living room, and his steps faltered a little.

"I'll tell her, you go handle that," I said, knowing deep down that this wasn't gonna end good.

His hesitation was clear in his body language, but he knew it was business before all else with us, so he walked out the door. When I walked into the living room B.J. was wide awake in Black Sam's arms, smiling like whatever baby gibberish she was talking was pure gold.

"If he's spoiled by the time I get there, I'm kicking your ass Samantha," I warned.

"No need to wait then, he's *too* adorable. You know I'm gonna spend every free moment with him, makes me want one of my own."

Hearing this comment caused me to look at Destiny, but I didn't find the panic I thought I would. In fact, it was the exact opposite, she was looking at her lady in a way I'd never seen her look at anyone. It wasn't just my son that was bringing joy to everyone around. For the first time, since we'd lost our father there was actually some good in all our lives that we could hold onto and enjoy. Knowing this didn't inspire more fear in me, but more determination. To get this shit finished, so we could live our lives. It's what Father God would've wanted.

"Angel, K.D. went to meet up with his people, which means it's about time to get this show on the road. Destiny, reach out to our local P.D. connect so we'll know when the Calvary has been called. Samantha, everything you need for little man is in those diaper bags by your feet. As soon as you get on that plane you're gonna have to be on that laptop monitoring everything. You're our eyes."

"I gotchu, don't worry, and as soon as we land. I'm taking this little cutie to the doctor to get whatever shots are necessary," Black Sam, replied.

"Do that because if *anything* happens to him, I'ma kill *all* of you," I said truthfully.

"Bone's comfortable, what else do you need?" Lil' Boy asked, walking up behind me.

"Take all the rest of the stuff, because you all are leaving in a minute. Make sure you grab the car seat by the door," I replied.

Everybody started moving around, helping to load up for the trip. I'd reclaimed my little man, because I needed more time with him. I'd never seen a more beautiful smile and it melted my heart as quickly as his daddy's touch.

"No matter what happens, I love you, B.J.," I whispered, kissing him repeatedly all over his face, much to his delight.

I felt the lump forming in my throat, but I fought it because crying wouldn't make shit any easier.

"Keep him safe," I said, handing him back to, Black Sam.

"I will, I promise," she replied, holding him close, walking out of the house.

I took the few minutes of silence to gather my thoughts, and center them on what was about to go down. I couldn't go into this battle like it was different, or with a mindset other than dealing out death by any means necessary. That was the only way to survive.

"You good sis?" Angel asked, putting her hand on my shoulder.

Moments later, I felt Destiny, do the same.

"Yeah, I'm good, but only because you two are with me. Nothing separates us again except the grave, agreed?"

"Agreed." Destiny replied.

"Agreed, but I ain't ready for all that. I got too much sex to have," Angel replied, laughing.

"I can't help you with that but killing Sapphire, will feel just as good."

Chapter 18
King Deuce

"Care to explain why the fuck we're way out here in Atlanta? Instead of back in Memphis, making somebody pay for what happened to your mom?" T.J. asked, as soon as I got out of the truck.

"Explain? When the fuck did I start having to explain myself, to you or anybody else?" I asked, knowing this bitch had lost her damn mind.

"The moment you started making bad decisions that could offset all of us. First you take off with only a handful of niggas, none of which are as capable as me. Then you send them back when you leave L.A. to fly down here. Come on, you're smarter than that, and you know there's a war going on."

"Yeah, I'm quite aware there's a war going on, because it was *my* mother that got killed. Let's keep shit one-hundred, though. You're madder that I left with Angel, than anything else. With that being the case you need to check your bullshit now, because she's the HBIC. You and I have had fun, true, but never misunderstand your position or your worth," I stated, coldly.

"My worth? I'd think you'd consider me priceless. Since *I'm* the goddamn reason you've still got dope moving in Tennessee, right now."

"The fuck are you talking 'bout?" I asked.

"I'm talking 'bout with the amount of bodies dropping, and the fact that your own mother was one of them. Mello, came around to check on things. Since your ass disappeared it was up to me to convince him everything was good, and no money would be fucked up. You're welcomed."

In the midst of all the drama, I had forgotten about the mufuckas I actually did need to provide again, that was *before* I got the pussy! Now my eyes were wide open to all of life's possibilities. Somehow controlling the streets of Tennessee, seemed small in the grand scheme of things. I'd never thought I would feel like this. Truthfully, I hadn't known I was feeling this way, until I'd spoken it aloud to Free, a little while ago. Niggas could say I was sprung or on some tender dick shit, but women like Angel, didn't come along everyday so they deserved holding onto.

"I appreciate what you did, to show you that I mean that. Once I'm finished down here, I'ma put you in charge back home."

"In charge? In charge of what?" she asked, with a confused expression on her face.

"In charge of the operation, what the fuck you think I'm talking about? I mean I know you're not affiliated, but you command respect so-."

"Wait, hold up, pause. You just finished telling me that little miss Angel is the head bitch in charge. Even if you were to turn shit over to me, what are you gonna do?" She asked.

"I got plans, don't worry."

"Plans-with Angel? You know it ain't safe around her and her sisters. Them bitches is radioactive and it ain't gonna get no better after all this shit goes down."

"We won't be around for the fallout, just accept the gift I'm giving you, and let's handle this wax," I said, using a gentler tone in hopes of defusing the situation.

"Whatever you say boss. What's the plan?"

"The plan is we've gotta secure not only a neighborhood, but a mile leading up to that neighborhood. We wanna make sure, once everyone walks into the trap, no one makes it out alive in the end."

"And how exactly do you plan to do that?" She asked, skeptical.

"You'll just have to wait and see, but I promise it'll be a show."

"Okay, so what are we waiting for?" she asked, pulling her Sig Sawyer 9mm from her waist and chambering the first round. We waiting on the phone call. What's the head count?" I asked, looking at the row of cars parked in the shopping center parking lot.

"We're twenty strong and everybody is strapped."

"Aight, well its customary for the general to talk to his troops before they go to war, so get everybody out," I ordered.

I wasn't about to sugarcoat shit for none of these niggas, they knew what it was when they started fucking with me. This situation was just the cost of doing business, no matter how personal it was. The sound of my phone going off had me reaching for it. I was kind of surprised to see that it was Free, already.

"What up sis?" I answered.

"It's time, I'm texting you the address. Put your people in position, then get here, this ends today."

Aryanna

Chapter 19
Destiny
Four Hours Later

"I just got the call. The F.B.I.'s hostage response team, along with the local swat team, and cops have been told to mobilize, but they're waiting on a location," I said, looking around the table at my sisters.

None of this surprised us, we'd always known the bitch was too much of a coward to come by herself. Plus, the feds wanted Free, in the worst way. Truthfully, they wanted all of us, and it damn sure wasn't for no day in court.

"Is everybody in place?" Free asked, looking at Angel.

"K.D. says we're a go and all the C-4 is wired."

"What about the escape routes?" I asked.

"Ours is airtight, K.D., and his people shouldn't have a problem backing out once all the chaos and shooting hits its peak. Just remember to tell him to take out that helicopter first," Free instructed.

We knew the law was coming with all the tricks of the trade, but they were the same old tricks. Sure, technology had improved over the years, and this particular group of law enforcement wanted us something fierce, but one thing remained the same. They couldn't fight what they couldn't see.

"You ready for this?" I asked Free.

"Ain't you?" She returned.

"I'm ready for it to be done," Angel said.

"Yeah, yeah, we know you got dick on the brain bitch. Just make sure you choose the right one," I cautioned.

"Shit, she's only had one so the choice ain't hard, no pun intended," Free said.

I opened my mouth to correct her, but the look Angel was giving me, said this wasn't the time for revelations.

"It's weird being back in this house," I said, changing subjects.

"I know right. Free you never did tell us why you had the old house rebuilt like new, but no one had ever lived here.

"Seems like a waste of money," Angel commented.

"Maybe it was. I just remember the last place we were all happy and innocent, and I wanted that to be preserved. I used to come here a lot and just sit out front, maybe trying to channel dad, or get some type of insight when a tough decision had to be made. That would've been hard to do if someone lived here, plus it could never be anyone's home except ours."

"Did Dad know?" I asked, softly.

"No, I never told him, I felt it would be a reminder of how he felt he'd failed us. You know he only had regrets when it came to that situation and how he handled it," Free replied.

It's Poetic Justice to end it here and now, but do you really wanna destroy the house?" Angel asked.

"It's time to move on. Besides, we all have something in life to hold onto that brings us happiness. It's best to let all the ghosts of the past die here and now."

In all my life I couldn't recall hearing Free, be so optimistic about the future. We'd lived good lives, but a lot of times it's hard to enjoy the spoils of war, when you had to keep one eye on the horizon, and the other on the hill you'd conquered. The way Free, was talking now had me convinced, she was finally ready to stop running and be the great mother we all knew she'd be. Maybe I'd take a page from her book.

"So, what about the neighbors because-."

My thought was interrupted by Free's phone going off, freezing us all in anticipation.

"It's her, she wants to know where to meet," Free said, already typing out her response.

While she was doing that Angel, was communicating with K.D. I pulled out my own phone to let Black Sam, know the curtain was going up and the show was about to begin.

"Five a.m. ready?" Free asked.

"She's monitoring all traffic cameras and relaying the info to K.D., so his people will know what's happening," I replied.

"Good, you two should go to your spots, take the houses across from each other," Free ordered.

Most mufuckas thought we were heartless, but we'd relocated every family on the block by using the excuse of a gas leak, so they wouldn't get caught in the crossfire. A more permanent solution would have to be figured out later though.

"I love you both," I said, standing up.

They followed my lead and we had a group hug before Angel and I headed out the back door.

"You go left, I'll go right, but remember we don't come out until Free, gives the signal," I said, before disappearing through the hedges, making a mad dash for my kissing spot.

It would seem our dear mother thought bringing the F.B.I. or national guard, was gonna save her ass, she was gonna learn today. For the next two hours we all sat and waited, texting back and forth, trying to remain calm. This was unchartered territory for us. Normally we brought the drama to mufuckas doors, fuck the wait. I was just becoming all the way impatient, when the group text went out that Sapphire was coming. A half an hour later, an all-black Escalade came creeping into the cul-de-sac, stopping several feet from the driveway to our family home. When the driver side door opened, time rewarded itself, I got a look at the mother I once loved. I'd wondered what I'd feel. Now I had my answer, I felt nothing.

Aryanna

Chapter 20
Freedom

"Well, well, well, I'm surprised you showed up, Sapphire, or should I call you Jewel Sky, now?"

"Where's my son?" She asked, impatiently.

I'm not sure what I expected when I finally came face to face with this bitch. The only way I could describe it was anti-climactic. Sure, I felt the rage and pain racing through me, but I still somehow expected more.

"You don't *have* a son, as far as I'm concerned. Now, my little brother, he's safe, and secure just the way my father wanted."

"I don't give a *damn* what your father wanted, you murdering bitch, I want-."

Her sentence froze in her throat when my pistol appeared, but I wasn't surprised. Like she said, I *was* a murdering bitch. I hated to get to the grand finale` so soon, which was why I'd approached her with only my cellphone in hand. Too late to go back now though.

"Why you so quiet now? Tell me how much of a murdering bitch I am. Better yet tell me how much I'm like you," I said, taking a step closer, until her nose was only inches from my gun barrel.

"He was gonna kill me and you *knew it.*"

"And you didn't deserve it? You and your F.B.I. buddies locked him up for a crime, you *knew* he didn't commit."

"What about the crimes he got away with? What about all the whores he fucked without remorse? He deserved-."

I don't know what she intended to say, but I wasn't letting her talk about my father like this. The vicious backhand I delivered with my pistol made that clear.

"You gonna lay there bleeding all day? Or, are we gonna finish this," I asked, sweetly.

"Ah, poor baby can't take the truth about her big, bad, daddy? Doesn't make him any less of a piece of shit. If you didn't have that gun I'd put you in a box with him," she spat, slowly rising to her feet.

I could feel my phone vibrating in one hand and my gun doing the same thing in my other. Ignoring the phone, I put it in my pocket, and tucked the gun into the waist of my shorts.

"I accept your challenge," I declared, firing a right-left combo that changed the location of her nose on her face.

I'd expected her to drop again, but she surprised me with two body shots, and a right cross, I barely escaped the full force of.

"You didn't think you were the only one with hands, did you?" She asked, smiling for the first time as she advanced on me.

I slipped her a jab and fired one of my own, adding more blood to her already gushing nose, following it with a gut punch that doubled her over. Even with the advantage I didn't advance though. I meant to *beat* this bitch.

"Shake it off *mom* and let's do this," I taunted.

"I'm-n-not-your mother,' she replied, gasping for air, but still coming towards me for more.

I faked with my left in order to deliver the knockout with the right, but I made the classic mistake of telegraphing my move which allowed her to catch me with an overhand left that felt like dynamite. There had already been blood, but now it was raining upon the asphalt, and it was mine. When I put my hand to my cheek I felt the gash in my face, but it wasn't until then, I saw the blade still dripping in between her fingers. Still I didn't reach for my gun, but instead squared up for another round.

"Free!" I knew that was Angel's voice, but it took Sapphire by surprise. Giving me all the time necessary to deliver a kick to her stomach, that would've made the actors in the movie 300 proud. She came clean off her feet, landing with a solid smack on her back, on the ground, and letting go of the razor.

"Free they're coming!" Destiny yelled.

It wasn't until then that my ears finally registered the sounds of a helicopter, but as soon as I looked to the sky it exploded into a bright orange glow.

"G-give me my s-son bitch!" Sapphire growled through clenched teeth, struggling to get her feet beneath her. By the time she made it to her feet she had a panoramic view of guns in her face.

"I told you before, you don't have a son. He's gonna be raised the right way," I said, cocking the hammer on my pistol.

"The F-feds have you surrounded. All you bitches are going down this time," she replied, smiling a bloody smile.

"If we do, you won't be alive to see it. You've gotta answer to Father God now."

With that we all fired at the same time, causing her head to explode like a dropped grapefruit. When her body fell I saw the first SUV bend the corner at a high rate of speed.

"We gotta go," I said, turning and running back into our old house. Once we were all inside I started counting to thirty in my head, while looking out the window to make sure as much of the Calvary was coming as possible.

"What the fuck are you waiting on?" Angel, asked from beside me.

"Patience little sister, patience," I replied, pulling my phone out.

"Patience my ass, bitch we gotta *go*," Destiny insisted.

When I reached my full thirty count I punched in the necessary numbers, within seconds the ground moved like an eight-point nine earthquake had suddenly hit. Followed by the dealing blast of every house on the block exploding. I had no doubts, the carnage would be epic. Just like I had no doubt, we were not the immediate problem anymore for the F.B.I. or police.

"Now we can go," I said, following my sisters out the back door, down to the lake that ran right up on our property.

Within minutes we were aboard the speed boat I borrowed with Destiny behind the wheel, headed away from the sounds of police cars, ambulances, and fire trucks. Now that it was all over, I couldn't deny the relief I felt flowing through me. I knew wherever my pops was he was smiling.

"K.D. says it's like shooting fish in a barrel," Angel, yelled over the boats engine, pointing at her phone.

I gave her a thumb up, knowing we were making a clean getaway, despite the odds being against us. It wasn't until now, I could let my mind switch gears to the two most important men in my life waiting on me. Knowing that now we could plan for forever. It took us ten minutes to reach the opposite side of the lake, ditch the boat, and make our way to the awaiting truck. Everything was going exactly according to plan, until K.D. pulled up in a truck behind ours.

"How the fuck-."

"I told him where to meet me," Angel said, giving me a sheepish look.

"Really? You pick now for this shit," I said, irritated by their bullshit.

"Listen, you know it was me who started that war by doing what I did in that club, and as a result Vontae's mom got caught up in-."

"What I know is that dude Monster started that shit when he tried to hit K.D. down here," I said.

"It doesn't matter who started it, we're gonna finish it.

It shouldn't take more than a few days, then I'll be on the first thing smoking out of the country," Angel said.

"Bitch are you *crazy*?! Do you know what the fuck we just did?" Destiny yelled, getting right in Angel's face.

"We sealed a much-needed score, with his help," Angel replied, pointing at K.D.

Suddenly all eyes were on me, awaiting my final say in this. I know Angel, felt a certain amount of loyalty to K.D., for all they'd been through, and because they were fucking now. That meant trying to fight with her could result in wasted time we didn't have, especially since I knew how stubborn this bitch was.

"Seventy-two hours to get it done and get out. If I gotta come back, K.D. dies. Agreed?" I asked, looking at Angel, then K.D.

I could tell she wanted to believe I was bullshitting. She knew better than that, and K.D. was smart enough to keep his mouth shut.

"Agreed," Angel said, hesitantly.

"Vontae remember what I told you, nigga," I warned, taking Destiny's hand, heading for our ride.

Aryanna

Chapter 21
King Deuce

Two Days Later

"You know, I'm starting to think, the only reason you kept me around is, so you could fuck my brains out," Angel said, smiling as she got out of bed, and walked naked to the bathroom.

From where I was laying the view was magnificent.

"Me? What about you, waking a nigga up in the middle of the night and shit. Where did you learn to suck dick like that anyway, you're supposed to be a virgin?" I asked.

"Don't get the shit slapped out of you, nigga. You know damn well, I was a virgin in every sense of the word when we met. That don't mean a bitch ain't watch *a lot* of porn, while I played with my pussy over the years. I studied them bitch's techniques."

"Yes, Lord, you *did*," I replied enthusiastically.

"Oh, don't think you won't be returning the favor, just as soon as you feed me," she informed me, coming back into the room, starting to get dressed.

"What you want to eat?" I asked, suggestively.

"Bojangles, so take your hand off your dick, get up, and put some clothes on so we can go."

"Yes ma'am," I replied, saluting her as I hopped out of bed to do as told.

Ten minutes later we were on the move. I didn't make it out of my parking spot, before T.J. stepped in front of my truck.

"What the fuck are you doing?!" I yelled, hitting my horn in hopes of moving her out of the way.

"Only what I'm paid to do," she replied, pointing to a car parked on her left.

The car door opened and right before my very eyes a ghost appeared.

"It-it can't be," I whispered in utter disbelief.

"What, who is that?" Angel asked.

"Mon-Monster," I mumbled, feeling bile rise instantly in my throat.

"Monster? That can't – that can't be, I *killed* monster, right?"

I wanted nothing more in the world than to agree with her. But, I was literally watching this nigga, step in front of my truck larger than life, full blown pissed. No sooner than I went to mash my foot on the gas, he held up what looked like a keyless remote, and pressed a button, immediately shutting my truck off, locking all the doors.

"What's going on Vontae, what the fuck is he doing?" Angel asked, panic starting to rise in her voice.

I didn't know the answer to that question. Even if I did, I wouldn't have been able to give it to her. I was focused on him. I'm not sure what I expected him to say, but what I didn't expect was the shit-eating grin now on his face.

"K.D. I—"

"Yo, Deuces, tell your mom, I said hello!" Monster hollered, before pressing another button. The delay gave me enough time to look at Angel's beautiful face, one more time. Then my truck exploded….

To Be Continued…
The Bossman's Daughter 4
Coming Soon

Preview of A Gangster's Revenge by Aryanna

Chapter 1
The Bells of Freedom

"See you around, Mitchell."

"Not on your life, motherfucker," I replied with a good-natured smirk and a firm middle finger salute as I strode out of the gates into the open arms of freedom. I didn't hear the CO's comeback, nor did I give a damn. I was out, I was finally out, and that meant I wasn't on anyone else's time except my own. I dropped my bag and took a moment to just admire the view of the unsettling, yet tranquil mountains in the distance. Unsettling because I'd been looking at those same sorry-ass mountains for the last four years of my sentence at Augusta Correctional Center. Today, this moment, was my last look, and that wasn't a promise. It was a guaranteed fact! I'd given the Virginia Department of Corrections twenty years of my life, and I refused to give them even one more, no matter what the cost or who had to pay it.

"Nigga, ain't you seen enough of these damn trees and the hillbillies that live in them?" she asked, eyes twinkling in the early morning sun with laughter and a hint of something livelier underneath. I gave her one of my seldom seen, but genuine smiles and scooped her off of her feet and into my arms.

"Boy, have I missed you, Light Skin," I said, kissing her with a loud smack on the mouth.

"I've missed you, too, Big Head. Now put me down so we can get the hell away from here." She didn't have to tell me twice as I sat her down, scooped up my bag, and strolled to the waiting car without a backward glance.

"Nice wheels for a college girl." I admired the 2021 E55 AMG Mercedes Benz.

"Well, you know, I do what I can, but it's time for an upgrade because this is last year's model."

"Damn, Kiara, is we getting it like that, yo?" I asked, running my fingers over the cherry-colored paint job.

"Big bro, you ain't name me Keyz for no reason." She opened the trunk so I could throw my bag in.

"Yeah, this shit fly. I thought shit would've been hovering by the time I got out of that muthafuckin' system."

"Don't trip, Big Head, you home now, and it's time to forget all that shit," she replied, pulling a black Samsonite suitcase from the trunk after I dropped my bag in.

Could I really forget what or who landed me there?

"Hello, earth to Devaughn!" Kiara said, waving her hand in my face. "I don't know where you just went, my nigga, but you need to stay out of those dark places. Shit, you scaring my girl."

I hadn't even noticed the badass light-skin chick exiting the car, but then again, it was impossible to see inside the car.

"Damn!" was all I could utter, looking at the gorgeous creature before me. She was no more than five feet, two inches with heels on and a body that screamed *fuck me*. The sun threw a blinding light off of the diamond dangling from her belly button, drawing my attention to her flat stomach and the tattooed tiger claws gripping her sides. I could tell she had a nice, juicy ass just looking at her from the front. Add to that her perfect breasts, long red-tipped dreadlocks and hazel eyes, and you had a specimen that would leave a certified pimp speechless.

"Dee, this is Candy Red." Kiara handed me the suitcase and snapped me out of my trance.

"Candy, this the nigga you been waiting your whole life to meet." She led her by the hand until she was standing in front of me. My sister wasn't no slouch either, standing at a respectable five feet, eight inches with her light honey complexion and enough body to make a gay man pause. I was standing in front of two of the most beautiful women I'd ever seen in my life, and I'd only been out of prison for five minutes! Whew, it was gonna be a long day.

"How are you doing, sweetheart?" I asked her, setting the suitcase down and reaching for her hand. The smile she graced me with was nothing short of amazing as she took the hand I offered and pulled me into a welcomed hug.

"It's nice to finally meet you, Devaughn. Or should I call you Dee?"

"Baby, you can call me anything you want, just as lon—"

"Oh nigga, please, you gonna fuck her. Damn!" Kiara laughed and pushed Candy back toward the open car door. All I could do was laugh.

"Come on, let's get the fuck out of here," I said, grabbing the suitcase and climbing in the backseat next to the still-smiling Candy.

"Oh, so I'm your driver now, nigga? Boy, you better be lucky I love your big-head ass or you'd be walking!"

"Yeah, yeah, just drive this big muthafucka before they change their mind and I wake up back in my bunk."

"Car start. Autopilot, navigate to the nearest bank from this location," Kiara said before turning around to face us.

"Ayo, this ride can do all that?" I asked in complete amazement.

"Yeah, nigga, it'd be a piece of shit if it couldn't. But that ain't the best part, this muthafucka tricked out on some 007 type shit. I'm talking fully bulletproof and everything. If a muthafucka get me in this car, then he had something nuclear." She diligently cracked a blunt while the car drove itself.

"So, cars drive theyself, but you still gotta roll your own blunt? Ain't that a bitch." I opened the suitcase to inspect its contents.

"Nah, I ain't gotta roll it. I want to. Besides, when you hit this fire-ass black diamond, you will appreciate me keeping it old school."

"Whatever," was my response as I pulled out some all-black Gucci jeans, a white Gucci t-shirt and some black and white Gucci high-tops to match. "What's this, Kiara? I told you to bring me some sweats."

"Alright, first, stop using my birth name, because you named me Keyz, and that's what I go by. Secondly, this is 2022 and that sweatpants shit is played out. Besides, nigga, I can afford to buy Gucci if I wanted to, so relax." She put the finishing touches on the blunt, but didn't light it. I didn't feel like arguing, plus it was her show.

"Just chill, Papi," Candy rasped into my ear while kissing a fiery trail down my neck. All thoughts of clothes were forgotten as her lips and tongue danced across my skin in such an incredibly sensual way that I had to remind myself to breathe. Dropping the clothes to capture her dreads, I brought her mouth to mine, where I experienced a kiss so powerful I was sure I heard electricity humming. Her tongue tasted of ripe kiwi and strawberries, and her lips held the soft moisture of plums. I could feel myself getting lost in her aura, in her essence, and I was helpless to stop it as I let my hands roam the exquisite landscape of her figure.

"Well damn, that kiss was so serious it got me hot!" Her voice broke me out of my trance, made me pull back and gaze deeply into the eyes of this remarkable young woman.

"It'll be magic," I whispered against her lips, letting her go and picking my clothes back up. The smile on Keyz' face said it all — I still had it. I could hear Candy's heavy breathing, and I could only imagine how wet her pussy was at that exact moment. This thought brought a smile to my face while I prepared to change out of the depressing khaki uniform the state of Virginia had issued me to come home in.

"Wait a minute, bro, you can do that while I run into the bank real quick. I need the suitcase, though, so dump the rest of that shit on the backseat."

The rest of that shit was a small arsenal of guns that I'd suggested she pick up for me. A quick inventory revealed a .45 with a 21-shot clip full of black talons, an HKmp5 submachine gun with two 60-round clips, a baby Uzi with two 60 clips, and a four-barrel glock with two 32-round clips. All in all, it wasn't a bad start.

"Good job." I handed the bag over the seat. Her response was to blow me a kiss on her way out of the car. I quickly stripped the loathsome khakis off me and started to dress in my new clothes.

"You know, we've probably got at least fifteen minutes before Keyz comes back," Candy said, licking those soft, red lips seductively.

"It shouldn't take her that long," I replied, sliding my t-shirt over my head.

"Trust me." She took the jeans from my hands and pushing a button to slide the partition up between the front and back seats, closing us off from the world. The car was spacious, sort of like a miniature Maybach, but I was still worried about time constraints.

"Maybe we shou—"

"Shhh, un-uh, just let me handle this." She made quick work of her clothes until she was completely and beautifully naked in front of me. Speech and thought took leaps out the window as I pulled her into my lap and locked onto the mouth I was beginning to crave more and more. Our kisses alternated between soft and sweet to a frenzy that displayed our wants and needs loud and clear. Without breaking contact, she slid around until she was straddling my pulsing manhood that was aching to spear her to any seat available.

"Candy, I don't have a – *oh shit!*" was all I could say to the feeling of her taking me inside of her juicy, warm pussy in one downward stroke. Her moans were instantaneous as she began a slow gallop that forced all the air from my lungs. I could hear the wetness of her delicious pussy with every motion, and the sweet smell of it was enough to make my mouth water. Gripping her waist directly opposite of the tiger claws, I guided her up and down faster and faster, feeling her stretch and mold herself to me until two became one. I felt my climax coming, and the speed of it frightened me.

"Wait. Candy, I'm about to— To—"

"Me too," she replied, retaking control of the situation by spinning around until she was throwing pussy and perfectly-shaped ass back at me in abundance. Silence was not an option as I roared like the lion I was, and we both found the promise land of blissful climaxes. I couldn't move, could barely breathe, and couldn't believe the still-shaking woman I was buried inside of had worked me so thoroughly.

"I demand a run back," I said, laughing and caressing one half of her fat ass.

"You're telling me. I've never came that fast for anyone," she replied, getting off my lap and sliding onto the seat next to me.

"How old are you, Candy?"

"I'm 26, why?"

"And you mean to tell me that some lil' young nigga ain't digging up in you every chance he can get?" This earned me a laugh and a twinkle of mischief from her mesmerizing eyes.

"I don't really fuck with dudes. It's mainly me and Keyz. Don't get me wrong, the sex is mind-blowing, but I always take a while to cum. Which means, Mr. Mitchell, that you and I are gonna keep doing this until we figure out the winning formula. If that's alright with you." She dipped her head and took me in her mouth without hesitation. Words weren't possible. All I could do was run my fingers through her hair while she took what she so obviously wanted.

"Mmmm, damn girl, save some for later."

"But I'm hungry, Daddy," she purred, going right back to her feast. The sound of the car door opening brought me back from the edge as Keyz hopped back behind the wheel.

"Y'all ain't done yet?" she asked with mock irritation. As much as I didn't want to, I had to tell Candy to stop so I could put the rest of my clothes on. Surprisingly, she didn't follow my lead.

"Get dressed," I told her, kissing her one more time.

"For what?" she replied, again pushing the button and letting down the partition separating us from the front.

"That's what I'm talking about," Keyz said, climbing into the back of the car and sitting next to Candy.

"Okay, so who's gonna drive this muthafucka?" I asked, taking the blunt and lighter she was passing me.

"Well, first we need to know where you want to go before anything," she said, tracing lazy circles around Candy's nipples with her fingernail. I hadn't thought about where to go first. I hadn't even decided if I would get straight to business or allow myself some down time before shit kicked off.

"Who knows I'm out?" I asked, lighting the blunt and inhaling deeply.

"Nobody for real. I've been doing like you said and telling anyone who'll listen that you set your time back again. You already know that the only people who check the Department of Correction's website is Dog and your uncle." Dog was my brother, and I trusted him, so him knowing I was out wouldn't be a problem. My uncle was a totally different story, but I'd deal with him when the time was right.

"How many soldiers do we have?" I asked, hitting and passing the blunt.

"I did a roll call this morning, and we've got 150 in the metropolitan area, 300 in Tidewater, Virginia, about 100 in Durham, North Carolina, and 70 in different parts of Texas."

"I see you've spread out quite nicely." I rubbed my chin and did the numbers in my head.

"If it ain't broke, don't fix it. It's EMU, bitch," she replied around a mouthful of smoke directed at Candy. EMU was our set. The movement had grown a lot in the last 10 years, but it was good because my team was on some real get-money shit. We weren't a bunch of broke-ass gangbangers like society had been trying to label us since the 60s. We'd moved past that into the business of being entrepreneurs like our founding fathers had originally envisioned, and I was proud of my contribution to that. Like my man Knuckles once told me, every day I made history.

"Do you know where Mikko is?" I asked, a bitter taste flooding my mouth at the sound of her name.

"Yeah, but— Are you sure you wanna start there? I mean, that's kinda obvious," Keyz replied, passing me the blunt back and running her hands up and down Candy's body in a slow, sensual way.

"I'm just trying to see my kids before life gets hectic. I owe them that, at least." I could feel the effects of the weed when I felt the anxiety and tension leap off me in waves, pushing me deeper into the comfortable leather seats. I knew I had to think things through, because everything begins and ends with the mental, and any miscalculation was a one-way trip to the grave. Like I said, prison was off the menu.

"Alright." Keyz reluctantly climbed back into the front seat and tossed the suitcase over. "Hey, Dee, tighten Candy up for me. She's looking a little horny back there." Candy took that as her cue and sent the partition back up.

"You ever made love on a million dollars?" she asked, opening the suitcase and dumping piles of money on the floor.

Aryanna

Chapter 2

Remember Me?

I watched the scenery change with unseeing eyes, allowing my mind to see the cities and towns we passed through like they were, once upon a time. Nothing was the same anymore, mainly because everything seemed to be made of steel, glass, and solar paneling. Don't get me wrong, it wasn't a bad thing that the world existed almost solely on natural resources and energy, but these were strange times in strange places for me. Two decades had changed a lot, and for the first time I felt every bit of my thirty-eight years. Candy's sleeping form stirred gently in my lap, causing me to look at her with a smile on my face. Our second encounter had been everything I promised her, and I showed her why sometimes age made all the difference in the world. Keyz had to turn the still-pumping classic Jay-Z up to deafening levels to drown out her girl's screams of pleasure and pain that hurt so good. I'd even caught her lowering the partition just enough to catch a glimpse of the rigorous workout I was putting Candy through. I guess it was too much for her, because it didn't take her long to shut it again. Looking back out the window, I saw the city of Centreville for the first time like it is now, and I wondered if my kids would be happy to see me. This day of freedom was long since talked about, but even though it was here, it still couldn't take away the years of pain I'd caused them. Nothing could.

"We've got a problem, Dee," Keyz said, accelerating fast around a corner and cutting the music off.

"What is it?" I asked, shaking Candy lightly and handing her clothes to her.

"There's an all-black Monte Carlo behind us, and it's been there since the bank."

"Cops?"

"No, I don't think it's the people because I haven't exactly been maintaining the speed limit, so they could've pulled us."

"What's the plan?" I asked, grabbing the HKmp5 and slamming a clip in it, setting it on full automatic.

"The plan is that I'm gonna drive us into this dead end around the corner and stop. After that, you know what it is."

By now Candy was dressed and loading the baby Uzi with a childlike grin on her face. Keyz turned the car around in the dead end and brought us to a stop facing the way we'd entered. I took a cigarette from the pack in Candy's hand, lit it, and watched as the Monte Carlo bent the corner hesitantly. Obviously not one to play waiting games, Candy opened her door, concealing her weapon, and waved the now-idling car forward. I admired her spunk, but her challenge didn't have the desired affect, because whoever it was just sat there.

"Back in the car, Candy," I said, opening my door and stepping out into the bright morning sun. I stood there with the door hiding my gun, smoking a cigarette as if I didn't have a care in the world, staring intently at the two figures in the car. Slowly, their car started to move forward, almost like it was being pulled by an unseen puppet master. I took a quick look around to see if any unsuspecting witnesses lurked about. Satisfied that I was reasonably safe, I took one last pull on my smoke and passed it to Keyz.

"Hold that, Light Skin, while I go talk to these nice gentlemen."

Chambering the first round into the gun, I stepped from behind the car door and opened fire. Bullets flew, glass shattered, and I heard the vague sounds of screams as I emptied the clip into the fast-fleeing car. I couldn't help but laugh, watching the driver sideswipe two cars and a mailbox trying to get away as fast as possible, knowing that whomever it was made a serious miscalculation that I'd be unarmed or timid. Climbing back into the car, I took the still-smoldering cigarette Keyz handed me and sat back while she smoothly guided us back to the main road.

"Who do you think it was, Dee?" Keyz asked, picking up her cellphone.

"If I had to guess, I'd say it was probably Rebekah and Renee's stupid-ass brothers, but I'm sure we'll know soon enough. Did you get the plates?"

"Yep, that's what I'm running right now. Why you so quiet Candy?" I asked, putting out the cigarette and turning to face her.

"I'm good," she replied, still holding onto the baby Uzi.

"I know you good, boo, but you're just quiet. I hope I didn't scare you," I took the gun from her hands and placed her hands in mine. I was searching her face intently for any sign that she couldn't be trusted, because loyalty was the name of the game we played, and anything that didn't fit the mold would be eliminated without questions.

"Scare me?" she laughed, scooting closer to me again. "Actually, you turned me on," she whispered, kissing me slowly and softly on the lips. She didn't know that I'd mastered my desires, especially those of the flesh, so I wouldn't allow myself to be controlled by lust. Her words sounded genuine, but I'd still keep my eyes on her and find out everything I could from Keyz before I made a decision on her fate.

"Last name Taylor." Keyz lowered the phone and looked at me with a question in her eyes.

"No, take me to Mikko's house."

She said something else into the phone before hanging up and driving on in deep thought.

"What is it, K?"

"I just think that we should eliminate them today. I can have it done while you're meeting with your PO later."

Damn, if the whole Taylor family disappeared on my first day home, I was guaranteed to cast the most suspicion.

They might even take me in for questioning. Monica Taylor was the reason I'd gone to prison in the first place, because as they say, "Hell hath no fury like a woman scorned." She and I were never a couple — more like friends with benefits. Then one day she drops a bomb on me and tells me she is pregnant. The baby wasn't the problem. The fact that she wanted me to leave my wife and other two kids, well, that was just plain unacceptable. Even as a young man, I was man enough to take care of my responsibilities, and I told her that our child would want for nothing, but somehow that wasn't enough. So when her demands of $10,000 were met with a not-so-subtle laugh and a fuck you, I found myself in handcuffs, facing a crime fit for the mind of a sexual deviant. All it took were three lying-ass little words from her juvenile sisters — "He touched me." — and my life as I knew it was over. My mind was made up then that they would pay, all of them, right down to the baby she claimed was mine.

"Do it," I replied harshly, contemplating the results of the actions in connection with the rest of my plans. I wanted to rush what had to be done because I fully intended to enjoy a lot of it, but plans were made to be followed, and I knew how things had to go.

"What's on your mind, Dee?" Candy asked, rolling another blunt with the speed and expertise of a veteran smoker.

"I got a lot on my mind, Red, and a lot of loose ends to tie up before the day is over."

"Don't even sweat all that, Papi, you know we got you."

"Is that right?" I asked, looking at her for the first time and wondering what was under the hood.

"Of course that's right. You lead, we follow until you tell or show us that it's our time to lead. You're Caesar and we're Rome, the new Rome, so just have patience and trust us, okay?"

Her statements set me back just a little, made me think of what could be lost or gained by trying to carry too much of the burden myself. I had to admit that she made sense, and I liked that.

"Baby, most people don't know it, but Caesar was quite gay. But I understand what you're saying and why you're saying it. Know this, though: be careful of how much intelligence you display, because it increases the levels of accountability dramatically. A wise man can play a fool, but a fool can't play a wise man."

"Very true, but see, I play my position, and my position for you is any and everything you need it to be. However, that only works if you know I'm capable," she replied, lighting the sweet-smelling ganja and inhaling mightily.

"Touché."

"Dee, we're here, and that looks like Latavia right there in the doorway." At the mention of my oldest daughter's name, I flung the car door open and stepped from the ride slowly so as to fully observe my surroundings. All I could do was stare in amazement at the beautiful young woman with her back toward me, thinking back to when she was just a little girl who hated to eat any type of vegetables. She was my secret Daddy's girl, the one who didn't really show it in front of me but was downright possessive when it came down to it. I laughed as I thought about the time she dragged a poor little girl by her hair because she felt I was giving the girl too much attention. That was my baby, the sneaky passive-aggressive one.

"I'll be back in time for dinner, Mom!" she yelled into the house, closing the door and immediately seeing me standing by the car. "Holy shit," she murmured, leaning against the door with her hand to her chest. She looked just like her mother did at that age, only slimmer and, from what I could tell, a lot fewer tattoos. At twenty-two, she was beautiful with eyes the color of warm chocolate and skin that looked like heated rosewood in the summer's morning light. The only thing missing was that megawatt smile that I knew she still had.

"Don't look so happy to see me." I walked up the steps and stopping right in front of her.

"It's— it's not that. I just can't believe you're out. I didn't think you were ever coming home," she whispered, trying to keep the tears in her eyes from falling. I didn't know what to say. How could I begin to explain the sacrifice I'd made for her, her sisters, and her mother all those years ago? Truthfully, I should've come home sixteen years ago, but when my wife got caught on a phone tap ordering the deaths of Monica's family, I did what I had to do. I couldn't let my six-month-pregnant wife go to prison, and so I did what was the unthinkable for my whole family: I took the charge. Now, standing in front of my oldest joy in the world, I knew that secret was better left buried.

"I told you they couldn't hold me forever. Can I get a hug?" I asked, extending my arms. And then the tears did fall as she stepped into my embrace, hugging me tightly to make sure I was real and not a figment of her imagination. I hugged her back as strong as I dared, not wanting to hurt her, yet not wanting to let her go either. "I missed you so much, baby girl," I told her, tears rolling soundlessly down my face.

"Me too, Daddy, I missed you, too."

It was time I faced the rest of my diva squad, as they were known.

"Come on, come back into the house for a little while." When I tried to steer us toward the front door, I met immediate resistance.

"Um. Dad, that's not really a good idea right now." I saw a touch of panic swim through her eyes, and I knew the reason for it.

"Trust me, sweetheart, I'm not looking for trouble." I signaled Keyz and Candy to join me. I could tell by the windbreaker that Keyz had slipped on that she was holding, and Candy still had her hands behind her back in her best innocent girl pose.

"Hey, Latavia, what's up?" Keyz stepped forward to give her a hug while Candy passed me the .45 that I tucked in the back of my jeans.

"'Sup, Kiara," she replied, sizing up Candy the whole time. "And you are?" she asked, stepping around Keyz until she was face to face with who she obviously felt was someone who didn't belong.

"I'm Keyz's girlfriend, Candy." She answered both the spoken and unspoken questions without hesitation or fear.

"La-La, come on." I pulled her by her arm so she could open the front door. It was no longer my right to walk into my baby's mama's house, and I respected that because no more fuel needed to be added to the inferno that we were.

"Are you sure, Dad?" she asked with her hand on the doorknob.

"Yeah, baby, I'm sure."

"Well, here goes nothing. *Mom!*" she yelled, opening the door and leading us into the house.

"What, Latavia?" Mikko yelled back, obviously agitated by something or someone.

"Dad's here."

"What the fuck is Damanya doing here?" she asked. I could hear her moving upstairs, coming toward us, but the staircase faced the back of the house.

"I said my Dad, not my sperm donor," Latavia replied testily.

"Devaughn?" Mikko rounding the corner suddenly. She was just like I'd remembered. Too vain to be taken hostage by gray hair without a fight, I admired her golden dreadlocks that just touched her shoulders. Her skin was still that dazzling light brown that reminded me of a sunset in some far-off land. The succulent mouth that stood agape was even more tantalizing now with the slight lines of age surrounding it than it had been all those years ago. After having five kids, she'd aged well and even slimmed down a little. But looks hadn't been her problem — fidelity had.

"Hello, Mikko." I stepped further into the house, allowing everyone in behind me so we could close the door.

"How— When— How did you get out?" she asked, flopping into the nearest seat, which happened to be in the living room.

"My time was up, or did you forget my max-out date?"

"I know, but you told me that you'd gotten more time for something."

"I just wanted to surprise everyone. Surprise." I moved past Latavia and taking a seat across from Mikko. She honestly looked like a beautiful deer caught in headlights, but I knew it wasn't shock as much as it was fear that had her looking at me so weirdly.

"Shit. I need a cigarette." She patted her empty pockets. I nodded toward Candy, who gave her a light before stepping over to stand beside my chair.

"And who are you?" Mikko asked in that polite nastiness that was her trademark. It was as if she'd just noticed there were other people in the room besides us.

"She's not your concern," I replied, taking the lit cigarette Candy offered me and pulling her into the seat next to me.

"Dad," Latavia growled at me with a look that said *be nice*. Mikko seemed to regain some of her composure, because she sat back on the couch and studied me with a fire in her eyes that I'd seen before. It was the fire of possession.

"Where's Day-Day and Deshana?" I asked, referring to my other two daughters Mikko and I shared. Sharday was twenty years old, and out of all of my girls, she was the biggest daddy's girl. I went in when she was only 13 months old, but the bond we had only grew stronger with time. Now Deshana, on the other hand, was my 18-year-old twin. She looked like me, acted like me, and much to the annoyance of her mother, she was just as smart as I was. All my children were intelligent. Latavia went to Georgetown, where she majored in criminal justice and was taking classes to become a lawyer. Day-Day was enrolled at Howard University, where she was the star of their music program. And now that Deshana had graduated, it was up to her where she went to school. All in all, I was very proud of my diva squad, because while they were all like me in some way, they'd succeeded this far without me.

"Well, let's see. Day-Day and Deshana are upstairs sleeping. And Jordyn — you remember her, right? — well, she's upstairs with her daddy." One look at Latavia and I could see the fear was back, as well as a silent plea for me not to lose my composure. I could tell Mikko was hoping to throw me off balance as I'd done her by bringing up the first child she had with another nigga while I was gone. Add to that that the nigga in question was upstairs sleeping like a baby and we were walking through Hell with gasoline drawers on. I caught Keyz giving me the *I wouldn't kill the nigga here unless he provoked me to* look

"And your son, how is he?" I replied casually, still smoking my cigarette. The fact I wasn't ruffled seemed to bother her even more, because the word *fine* came out in a deep growl as she puffed away on her cigarette. I couldn't help but smile. "La-La, will you go wake your sisters up so I can take you all to breakfast?"

Without a word, she got up and started toward the stairs.

"Oh, don't forget Jordyn," I said, never taking my gaze from the now bug-eyed face of my ex-wife.

"Daddy," Latavia said again in that voice that told me I was pushing again.

"It's only fair, Latavia, now go ahead," I replied, putting my cigarette out. "Would you like to join us, Mikko?" I asked, all innocence and charm.

"It seems you have quite enough company as it is. Besides, I don't want you to spend your whole little $25 check in one spot," she replied, smirking.

"That reminds me. Candy, run out to the car and bring me ten apiece for the kids, all five of them." I smacked her ass for good measure and caught the mischief dancing in Keyz's eyes.

"Ten? Wow, big spender," Mikko kicked her feet up on the chipped wooden coffee table. I didn't respond. Instead I looked around at what could have been a nice house if the right decorations were applied. The living room was spacious with wall-to-wall carpeting, but the oversized couch and entertainment center made it look like a cluttered mess. It was clean, though, which I guess was all that mattered when you were on a fixed income. Maybe she'd be able to do more once I moved the girls into their own spot.

"Daddy!" screamed my two girls in unison as they came flying down the stairs and hopped into my lap.

"Damn, y'all got huge on me," I replied, hugging them tightly. My little girls had grown into not-so-little women and filled out enough to make me glad I was carrying a big gun.

"When did you get home, Dad?" Day-Day asked.

"About two hours ago, actually. Come on, you should've already knew where my first stop was going to be," I replied, looking back and forth between my two beautiful women.

"We thought you still had more time to do," Deshana whispered, tears clouding her eyes and spilling over onto her face.

"Come on, baby, don't cry. I'm home now, and I'm not going anywhere."

"Oh, you're going somewhere, nigga, because you ain't staying here," Craig said, coming down the stairs wearing sweatpants, some boots, and a grin on his face. It was at this moment that Candy came back in with the money I'd sent her to get, and the look on her face told me the tension in the air was evident.

"Are you even allowed to be here, nigga?" Craig asked, sitting next to Mikko and putting a possessive arm around her.

"Daddy, don't," Latavia said, obviously seeing the anger and hatred flash in my eyes. Mikko saw it, too, because she put her hand on his knee and whispered something to him.

"You girls go get dressed so I can take you out to eat," I said softly, pushing them from my lap.

"Who said they was going with you?" he asked like he had all the rights in the world to say anything to me about my children. Nobody moved. It seemed like no one was breathing.

"Craig, this ain't what you want," I replied calmly.

"Girls, you heard your father, now get dressed." Keyz led them quickly from the room.

"What, am I supposed to be scared of you because you was in the pen, muthafucka? You was in there for some pussy shit, for touchin' on—"

He never finished his sentence before I was out of my seat with my .45 smiling sweetly in his face.

"Go ahead, say it, you bitch-ass nigga, and you'll die right here, now. Go ahead, I bet you won't say it. Matter fact, open your mouth, bitch." I cocked the hammer on the pistol and shoved it savagely between his teeth. "These are the crimes I got away with, nigga! I murdered pussies like you in these streets, so you best remember that and me, because the next time I see you, it's the last time I see you." I was so mad I was shaking, and I could hear the gun barrel rattling around against his teeth. I wanted to kill him, I wanted to blow a nice hole through his head. And I probably would've if I didn't see her standing there with her big doe eyes looking at me, almost through me.

"Please don't shoot my daddy," Jordyn whispered. I had every right to kill him, but I wouldn't do it in front of his little girl. Maybe someday a nigga would grant me that courtesy.

"Mikko, I suggest that you tell your boyfriend, fiancé, or whatever the fuck he is that I'm not the one." I looked at her squarely before taking the gun out of his mouth. I could tell two things when I looked at her: one, she was scared for her own life, and two, it turned her on in a way that nothing had in twenty years. She'd done things, horrible things, in order to forget the love she had for me and hopefully the reason why she loved me. As she licked her lips and slowly shook her head, I could tell she hadn't forgotten shit, She remembered exactly what it was.

Chapter 3

Am I a Monster?

The car was full, but the conversation was strained. Nobody really wanted to comment on what happened back there, but at the same time, no one except Jordyn knew what really happened. The inevitable question came.

"Daddy, what did you do when we went upstairs?" Latavia asked quietly. I'd been gone a long time, and that's why Day-Day and Deshana only had stories of me for most of their memories, but Latavia was old enough to remember my anger and how nothing good ever came from that.

"Does it matter?" I asked, looking out the window at the cars on the highway.

"Dad, don't be like that, because you've always promised us honesty."

I knew she was right, just like I knew I'd have to tell them the truth when they came back downstairs and saw Jordyn holding onto her father like he might disappear any moment. I was mad at myself for losing my temper like that, but I couldn't take it back now.

"You girls aren't babies anymore, so I'm not gonna treat you like you are. What I will tell you is don't ever ask me a question that you don't want the answer to. I've tried to keep you ignorant of me and the things I'm capable of, but if you insist on asking me, I'm not gonna lie about it. So, I ask you: do you want an answer to that question, Latavia?" I looked directly at her for the first time since we'd gotten in the car. I could see the uncertainty in her eyes, but she was my daughter, and I knew she wouldn't back down.

"Yes," she replied in a strong and clear voice.

"Keyz, where are we going to eat?" I asked.

"We're going to Old Country Buffet in Manassas, and we'll be there in about ten minutes." I didn't know exactly what I planned to say, but I figured ten minutes would cover it.

"Candy, pass me the suitcase back here. I'ma show you girls what my life really consists of so there won't be any questions about your father as a man," I told them, opening the suitcase so they could see the money and guns. Then I took the .45 from out of the back of my jeans and sat it on my lap. "I put this gun in Craig's mouth with the intention of blowing his muthafuckin' head off for disrespecting me, but Jordyn asked me not to shoot her dad, and I didn't. In my world, disrespect is not tolerated, but I tried to let it go on the strength of your mother, mainly. Dude somehow felt that I was some type of bitch, and I reacted accordingly. I'm a member of one of the most ruthless criminal organizations that've ever existed in the known world, and I take that very seriously, but what you see before you is only a small part of everything. I've been out of prison for three hours, and I'm riding around in a million-dollar car with a million in a suitcase and a few toys to keep me company. So, to sum this little speech up, I'm your father, and I love you more than life, but I'm also a gangsta with a lot of responsibilities." I was honest and to the point, and they would either love me or hate me for it.

"Have you killed someone before?" Deshana asked in a surprisingly calm voice. At first all I did was look at her, trying to gauge whether or not she could handle the truth.

"Yeah," I replied simply, choosing not to elaborate because now was not the time for glorifying or trading war stories.

"Dad, we've always known that you loved us and you wouldn't do anything to hurt us, so my question is are we in danger because of the life you lead?" Day-Day asked, looking back and forth between me and the suitcase.

"No," Keyz said from the front seat. "So far your father's activities have been restricted to the inside for obvious reasons, and the only one operating on his orders in these streets is me. I've been careful in making sure that our life hasn't spilt over into yours, which is why I don't get to see you as often as I'd like."

"You're part of this too, Kiara?" Latavia said with obvious disgust.

"Yeah," she replied, looking directly at Latavia in the rearview mirror.

"So what the fuck are we supposed to be, some type of criminal family now? The only reason I went to school to become a fucking lawyer is because you were taken away from us for some complete bullshit, but now I see that I'm probably still gonna end up defending your ass in court anyway!"

No one said a word. Everyone just waited to see what my reaction was gonna be to her rants and accusations.

"I am what I am, Latavia, and I've never claimed to be perfect. The only thing I've ever claimed to do is love you unconditionally. Can you do the same?"

Everyone was looking at her, waiting and wondering what, if anything, could be agreed to as we pulled into the parking lot of the restaurant. I'd taken off my mask and revealed the boogieman underneath, but I didn't know if that was the right decision now. I saw the pain in my daughters' faces, the uncertainty of what I was really capable of and if the sins of the parent would someday be visited on them. A promise that would never happen would seem hollow to my ears, so all I could do was wait.

"I love you, Dad — unconditionally. Just promise that you'll do your best to protect the family and yourself now that you're home." She curled up on my lap like she use to when she was little.

"I promise you that, and I also promise that no matter what happens, I'ma keep on loving you. Now, I'm starving, so can we eat, please?" I asked, opening the door and closing the suitcase before getting out of the car.

We all piled out of the car and stormed the restaurant like a group that hadn't eaten in years. We spent the next two hours laughing, joking, and enjoying both the food as well as the company, and for once forgetting the pain of the past. I knew it was the little moments like this in life that I'd have to hold on to when the coldness of my life became too much for me to bear. I'd never been one to seek happiness because I'm a firm believer that contentment works just fine, or satisfaction as the least, but right there I was actually happy for the first time in a long time. In the back of my mind, I still knew a lot of people had to die, but even that didn't sadden me.

"Candy, you still got that?" I asked, referring to the money from earlier. She passed me three stacks under the table with a wink and a smile in my direction. "Alright, ladies, so this is what it is. I'm home now, and the means that you all no longer have to worry about anything." I handed them each a stack of money. "That don't mean that you're not gonna finish school or that you won't start school, Deshana. What this means is that I'm gonna help you in any way that I can, and for starters, I think it's time you all got your own place."

"Now, Dad, when you say our own place, do you mean individually or one house together?" Day-Day asked, doing a quick count of the $10,000 in her hand.

"Separate, fully-furnished apartments until you finish school, and then we'll go from there. But if you think niggas gonna be running in and out, you got the game fucked up, and I hope you know that."

"What if I said I wanted to be a part of the movement?" Deshana asked quietly, causing the whole table to go silent.

"Excuse me?" I replied, not sure I heard her right.

"What if I said that I was ready and willing to be a part of your world, Dad?"

"What makes you think you're built for that?" I asked, slowly sipping my orange juice.

"I'll show you." She leaned over and whispered something to Candy. I couldn't hear what they were heatedly discussing, but the look Candy gave me said there was an obvious problem.

"Keyz, you, Day-Day, and Latavia go to the car now," Candy said without taking her eyes off of me.

"But—"

"Don't. Just go, Latavia," I said, holding up my hand to silence whatever argument she was planning to give.

"Dee, go ahead and pay the bill and follow them to the car."

I scanned my surroundings, still not spotting whatever danger Deshana had obviously located with an untrained eye.

"I'm not going anywhere. Which one of ya'll got a gun?"

"Dad, we can handle this, and you don't need to be in here right now," she replied, flashing me my own four-barrel glock from the suitcase.

"Sneaky muthafucka." I got up and made my way to the counter.

When I got there, I finally saw them in the booth, sitting there like nothing was wrong. All I could do was shake my head and laugh, because I could only wonder what was going through Craig's mind as he sat there with his homeboys. One thing was for sure: he wouldn't be expecting whatever was coming next. Without looking back, I walked out of the restaurant and slid into the backseat of the waiting car. As soon as I got in, three pairs of eyes drilled me with expectant looks, and I noticed that Keyz was now holding the baby Uzi like a life preserver.

"What's going on, Dad?" Latavia asked first.

"I don't know, but I'm confident that your sister can take care of herself."

No sooner had I uttered the words than I heard Candy's voice saying "Pop the trunk." The car sunk down on its springs a little as we took on more weight. I knew that feeling — there were definitely at least two bodies in the trunk. I hid my grin behind the blunt that I was struggling to light while Candy and Deshana hopped in the car without a word.

"Let's go," I said to Keyz, inhaling heavily on the weed and holding the smoke until it felt as if my lungs would collapse.

"So, are we supposed to act like nothing happened?" Latavia asked with obvious and blatant annoyance.

"Yeah." Deshana took the blunt from my hand and hit it twice before passing it to Candy so she could blow her a shotgun.

"Witnesses?" I asked reluctantly.

"None," Deshana said, choking on all the smoke in her lungs and coughing mightily.

"That ain't no dirt weed, slim," Keyz said, signaling for the blunt next.

"How many?" I asked.

"All of them," Candy replied, lighting a cigarette and passing it to me. These two pint-sized women had abducted three niggas in broad daylight without there being one witness to the crime, and that was quite a job. On top of that, they were as cool as the other side of the pillow.

"You know that still don't prove shit, right?" I asked Deshana, passing her the cigarette. Her smile caused me to shiver a little bit. For a split second, she looked exactly like me twenty years ago.

"What the fuck you mean *what happens next*, Deshana? What happens next is that our dear old dad is gonna take us the fuck home before we inadvertently get caught up in some shit. Ain't that right, Dad?" she asked, fixing me with a stare that said *remember your promise to keep us safe.* I knew she was right, and I wasn't about to argue with her all day.

"Keyz, how much time before the PO thing?"

"We've got about five hours before her office closes, but we could always show up at her house," she replied, smiling and passing the blunt back over the seat.

"Nah, too early for house calls. Let's drop Latavia and Day-Day off at the house real quick."

"What about Deshana?" Latavia asked.

"Deshana, how old are you?" I asked, passing her the blunt and taking my cigarette back.

"Dad, you know I'm 18. My birthday is tattooed on your hand."

"Yeah, I know how old you are, but for some reason your sister has forgotten that you're grown, so I was asking for her benefit."

"Deshana, you can't be serious. You're just— you're just gonna go with him?"

"Latavia, this *him* is our father, and you muthafuckin' right I'm going with him. Look, sis, I love you, and you know that, so just trust me. Dad ain't gonna do shit to hurt me, and deep down you know that, too."

It seemed as if we were at a crossroads again, but I knew this time it was between them and not me. My children had grown up and developed minds and opinions of their own, and as their father, it was my duty to let them think for themselves.

"Dad?" Latavia said, looking at me with her heart in her eyes.

"What is it that you want me to say, La-La? I've never forced right or wrong on you, only the reality that you will have to live and suffer with the consequences of both. Would you prefer I was a hypocrite and said that it was okay for me and your aunt to be Bloods, but none of you can? Do you remember when you were little and didn't want to eat your vegetables? What did I use to tell your mom?"

"That you didn't eat them, so we didn't have to either," she replied with a reluctant smile.

"Do as I say, not as I do has never been real good in my parenting book, unless the situation was extreme. And before you say anything, know and understand that I ain't never killed a nigga who didn't deserve to die."

"La-La, I just want to spend some time with Dad, okay? Don't trip. I'm still gonna be the same loveable me in the morning who listens to you and your boyfriend make kissy faces over the phone." She laughed at Latavia's sudden blush as she looked directly at me.

"Trust me." I pushed a piece of hair that escaped from her ponytail back behind her ear as the car came to a stop in front of their house. "You okay, Day-Day?" I asked, turning to face my one child who'd been silent for the whole ride.

"I'm fine, Daddy, I'm just glad you're home." She slid over to give me a hug and a kiss.

"Give your mom this money and tell her to call Keyz if she needs anything," I said, opening the door and stepping out of the car. I could hear our guests getting restless in the trunk. "Keyz, turn the music up. Listen, girls, if anyone asks where you got money from, tell them you got it from your aunt. It's still a secret that I'm home, so don't tell nobody until I let you know."

"Alright, Dad, I love you," Day-Day said, giving me another hug and walking toward the house.

"I love you too, baby. Come on, La-La, give me a hug. You know you want to." I wrapped my arms around her.

"Daddy, just be careful, please," she murmured against my chest, holding onto me like I might blow away in the breeze.

"I got you, babe," I said, kissing the top of her head and watching her go in the house as I climbed back in the ride.

"Alright, now what?" I asked my entourage of three.

"Well, apparently this is now Deshana's show, because she's informed me of what she needs and why she needs it," Keyz said, pushing the car at a fast clip.

"So, what's the deal, Lil' Me?" I'd been calling her Little Me since she was born, and as it turned out, I might've been more right than I knew.

"We're going out to Keyz's spot so I can have a nice chat with these gentlemen, and when that conversation is concluded, I guess you and I will have a talk too, Dad."

Candy was silent, but the words behind her eyes said enough.

"You agree, Candy?"

"I do. I think that since she spotted the threat, she should be the one to talk to our friends in the trunk first."

I guess I was out-voted, but this was an opportunity to find out how sound Candy's judgment was and what Deshana was made of. Her following in my footsteps wasn't an ideal plan, but I was a firm believer that my kids wouldn't learn how to do wrong the wrong way. I lost a lot of homies growing up because their parents chose to show willful ignorance and left it up to the streets to teach their children. In the end, those same parents were taught how unforgiving and merciless the streets could be, but the cost of that lesson was a high price to pay. Sitting back in my seat, I enjoyed the ride as we left the city and ventured into the country. The scenery was nice and relaxing, but I couldn't really enjoy it because Keyz was pushing the shit out of the car.

"Ayo, drive like you know it's three niggas in the trunk."

"Boy, please, I got this. I told you this muthafucka was tricked out. What, you think I ain't got radar?" she asked, pressing down harder on the gas pedal.

"Okay, Miss Radar, but if the peoples sneak up on us, then it ain't gonna matter, because I'm shootin'."

All she did was laugh at me while motioning for Candy to climb into the front seat with her.

"Before I forget, is everything set up for that other situation later on?"

"Yeah, all I've gotta do is make the call when you're at your PO's office, because the house is already under surveillance."

"I was thinking, it might be kinda risky snatching that many people, so we might need more than just a few guys for this."

"Already ahead of you. That's why we already had someone take the four main targets, since they lived together, and the rest will be picked up separately. Nobody disappears until you have that alibi, though."

"Do you think we could hold the main ones on ice? I kinda wanted to do them myself." I could tell by the disapproving look she was giving me that wasn't a good idea. At the same time, I knew she could respect how personal it was for me.

"Are you sure?"

"Yeah, I'm absolutely positive."

"Fine, I'll make it happen. I'll have them brought to the house now." She picked up her cellphone, still not changing the disapproving look on her face.

"Who are you talking about, Dad?"

"You'll see," I answered, smiling a smile of sweet satisfaction and long overdue justice. We made the rest of the trip in a comfortable silence, only slightly interrupted by the welcome sounds of the *Miseducation of Lauryn Hill* leaking through the speakers. My mind constantly jumped back and forth between past and present and occasionally went on into the future. For me, it wasn't so much about what the future held as it was to actually have a future. Twenty-five years ago, I would've bet everything I had and ever dreamed of having that I wouldn't see thirty-eight years old. Saying thirty-eight was like saying ninety or 100 back then, but I'd made it, and now I had my sights set further down the line.

"We're here," Keyz announced, climbing from the car and going to the trunk. Candy stood next to her with the baby Uzi, and Deshana took up the other side with the HKmp5. Since this wasn't my show, I just stepped back and watched my three beautiful and very dangerous ladies work their magic.

"Okay, you stupid muthafuckas, get the fuck out of my car!" Keyz yelled, sticking a pearl-handled 9mm berretta in Craig's eye socket. I could tell he wanted to say something, wanted to cuss and scream and make empty threats, but he hadn't figured out whether he'd live or die yet. He couldn't roll the dice all the time.

I left them to the work of herding the cattle, so to speak, and I turned around to admire Keyz's big-ass house. There was green grass as far as the eye could see and three different fountains spread around the driveway, spraying some of the bluest water imaginable. I couldn't see any other houses around us, just wide open land and something like a smaller version of the main house off in the distance. I didn't know what to say. My twenty-four-year-old little sister was living in a fucking mansion! A smile creased my face when I walked up the stairs and through the doors that seemed to open like magic from a movie set.

"Shit," I mumbled, walking into the foyer and immediately noticing the twin staircases that seemed like they were only one step below the clouds. The roof was made of glass allowing the sun to throw blazing rays off of the rose-colored marble floors that surrounded me. Looking up, I saw the biggest chandelier I'd ever seen, and with the sunlight moving through it, rainbows bounced everywhere. It was too much. This was the type of house seen on TV or in the magazines, but not in the life of a hustler — unless it was Frank Lucas.

"Welcome home, Mr. Mitchell," said a petite Spanish woman who materialized from nowhere.

"Thank you."

"My name is Tara, and I work for you and your sister. Would you like me to show you to your wing of the house?"

"My wing?" I asked slowly, still not believing that my baby sister was living like Bruce Wayne by day and Rayful Edmonds by night.

"Yes sir. If you'll just follow me to the elevator." She turned and walked underneath the staircase. The wall opened up and we stepped aboard the elevator for the brief ride to the top of the house. "You'll be staying in the north wing." She made a right out of the elevator and escorted me through a twenty-foot archway that boasted doors with EMU engraved into the wood. Behind the doors stood a spacious hallway with thick red carpet that looked like it easily stretched for a quarter of a mile.

"What's the layout of the house?" I asked, still following her lead.

"There are twelve bedrooms, six in each wing. Ten and a half baths, a swimming pool, library, movie theater, full gym equipped with weights and a regulation basketball court, a conference room that seats twenty, and an indoor sauna and Jacuzzi. Now, you probably noticed the miniature house down the way a little bit. Well, that's for parties and entertainment purposes, because Ms. Keyz don't like everybody up in her shit."

"Understandable. I notice that there's clothing in the other rooms we've passed. Who's staying there?" I asked, coming to a stop behind her at the door to the master suite. Tara graced me with a smile that went all the way to her beautiful gray eyes, but she said not one word and simply opened the double doors in front of us. An enormous king size bed sat front and center when we walked through the doors. The color scheme of the room was harmonious shades of black and red, matching and complementing the plush carpet beneath my feet. Two nightstands the size of coffee tables surrounded my bed, and the matching armoires were posted to my left next to the windows. I could see into my bathroom, where my Jacuzzi tub sat filled with bubbles and black rose petals, and suddenly the sounds of Jaheim escaped from somewhere hidden. To my immediate right was my walk-in closet filled to capacity with clothes and shoes from labels and designers I'd never heard of, but the quality of the product was evident.

I took all this in with one smooth swing of my head from left to right, but the sight of the things on my bed caused me to pause and rub my hands across my face to conceal my excitement. Before me were five young women in various shades, shapes, and ethnic backgrounds, but every one of them was breathtaking and almost completely naked.

"Close your mouth, nigga, damn." Keyz pushed me in my back and laughed.

"What is this, K? Don't get me wrong, because I'm down for whatever, but— Mmm, damn, am I ever gonna get some sleep?"

"Nigga, you told me that it didn't matter where we lived as long as we were together and I kept 'options' around the house. Meet options." She pushed me all the way into the room.

"Mmm, damn, you're a sexy muthafucka," said a four foot, nine inch dark chocolate angel, running her hands underneath my shirt and then pulling it over my head.

"You not too bad yourself, baby," I said huskily, taking her hand and watching intently as she did a slow twirl, showing off her firm, plump ass.

"Hold up, DC." Keyz stopped me from being led to the bed where the rest of the women patiently awaited my arrival.

"What?" I asked, throwing a confused look at my sister.

"We got bidness to handle, nigga. Come on, stay focused. DC and the rest will wait 'til later, won't you, ladies?"

"Yes, Daddy," they replied in the sexiest harmony since Destiny's Child.

"DC stands for Dangerously Chocolate," she said, licking lazy circles around both of my nipples and squeezing my crotch lightly.

"Oh shit. Come on, Keyz, because in a minute there ain't gonna be no turning back." I walked out of the room and back down the hallway in a daze.

"Damn, nigga, do you want your shirt?" she asked, walking behind me, laughing hard.

"Nah, I ain't trying to get blood on it, anyway," I replied, holding the elevator door.

"You ready?" she asked, pushing a button.

"I've got twenty years of pent-up rage to unleash. Ready? Trust me, you don't even know the half of it."

The doors opened onto a brightly-lit basketball court where a rigorous game of five-on-five was taking place.

"Everybody on the court has rank and position, but you'll meet them later." Keyz led me through a side door.

The room we walked into was cold, and not just temperature-wise. It was cold. I'm sure I didn't even want to know half the stories these walls could tell. The room was bare except for two sets of running lights overhear, a cooler with some tools leaning against it, and three bodies strapped to three chairs. Deshana stood next to the gagged men, pistol in hand, and a look of determined violence on her face. Walking toward her, I noticed the large drain directly under Craig's chair and the pleading look in his eyes.

"Don't look at me. I'm just a spectator in all this." I took the chair Keyz offered me.

"Being that I know you have a lot to do, Dad, I don't want to waste a lot of time," she said, chambering the first round into a chrome .44.

"Nice gun."

"Thanks. Now then, I don't know you two muthafuckas, so you're really of no importance to me. I just want you to know that this is all Craig's fault." With that, she stepped to the guy on her left and shot him twice in the face.

"It's okay, boo," she told the second man, who was screaming for all he was worth behind the gag in his mouth. "Look at me. It's okay, I promise," she said sweetly, placing the gun under his chin and squeezing the trigger. She killed with the clinical detachment of a professional, making me wonder if this was her first kill. I felt my pulse quicken while watched my daughter work, watched the same beast that lived in me come to life in her and, for a moment, I was actually disturbed.

"Keyz, I need that special brew." She stuck the gun in the back of her hip-hugging jeans and pulled the gag from Craig's mouth.

"Deshana, what the fuck is wrong with you?" he screamed with spit, tears, and snot racing down his face.

"My dear Craig," she said, punching him hard enough to draw blood from his mouth.

"I've done nothing but treat you right, Deshana. Please don't do this. Think of Jordyn."

"Jordyn, Jordyn. Did you ever think about me, Craig? Do you ever stop and consider how you treating me like I was worthless because my last name is Mitchell made me feel? You could never take that my mother loved my father more than any nigga she's ever been with! And you took that out on me, you sorry motherfucker. Guess what? It's my turn now. Hey, Dad, I got some old-school flavor for you." She walked behind Craig and snatched his head back. I saw the glitter of steel in her mouth, and I knew what was coming. "Smile forever, bitch!" She pulled the straight razor from her mouth and sliced him from mouth to ear on both sides of his face. That wasn't the worst part. When she let his hair go and slapped him on his cuts, his face opened up like a pussy, and while he screamed I could see his teeth through the side of his jaw. I thought now would probably be the time she put a bullet in his head, but when Keyz came back carrying a pot that was still boiling, I knew the situation was serious.

"Deshana."

"I got this, Dad." She took the pot and gloves and walking back toward her barely-conscious victim. "Last, but not least, the fun part." She laughed as she raised the pot and poured boiling, black oil all over Craig. I'd never heard anyone scream like that, and I'd only seen a look of murderous glee like that on one other person — me. The scalding oil peeled Craig's face off from eyebrows to chin and sent it down the drain with inhuman amounts of blood.

"Finish it," I said, lighting a cigarette to mask the smells of shit and piss that Craig reeked of.

"Goodnight, Craig," she said sweetly, dumping two bullets into the back of his head.

**A Gangster's Revenge
Available Now!**

The Bossman's Daughters 3
Coming March of 2018

Raised as a Goon 4

By Ghost 3/15

A Drug King and his Diamond 3/19

By Nicole Goosby

Bred by the Slums 3/25

By Ghost

Who Shot Ya 3/31

By Renta

BOW DOWN TO MY GANGSTA

By **Ca$h**

TORN BETWEEN TWO

By **Coffee**

BLOOD STAINS OF A SHOTTA II

By **Jamaica**

WHEN THE STREETS CLAP BACK II

By **Jibril Williams**

STEADY MOBBIN

By **Marcellus Allen**

BLOOD OF A BOSS **V**

By **Askari**

BRIDE OF A HUSTLA III

By **Destiny Skai**

WHEN A GOOD GIRL GOES BAD II

By **Adrienne**

LOVE & CHASIN' PAPER II

By **Qay Crockett**

THE HEART OF A GANGSTA III

By **Jerry Jackson**

LOYAL TO THE GAME **IV**

By **T.J. & Jelissa**

A DOPEBOY'S PRAYER II

By **Eddie "Wolf" Lee**

IF LOVING YOU IS WRONG... III

The Bossman's Daughters 3
By **Jelissa**

BLOODY COMMAS **III**

SKI MASK CARTEL II

By **T.J. Edwards**

BLAST FOR ME **II**

By **Ghost**

A DISTINGUISHED THUG STOLE MY HEART **III**

By **Meesha**

ADDICTIED TO THE DRAMA **II**

By **Jamila Mathis**

LIPSTICK KILLAH II

By **Mimi**

THE BOSSMAN'S DAUGHTERS 4

By **Aryanna**

Available Now

(CLICK TO PURCHASE)

RESTRAINING ORDER **I & II**

By **CA$H & Coffee**

LOVE KNOWS NO BOUNDARIES **I II & III**

By **Coffee**

RAISED AS A GOON I, II & III

By **Ghost**

LAY IT DOWN **I & II**

LAST OF A DYING BREED

By **Jamaica**

LOYAL TO THE GAME

Aryanna

LOYAL TO THE GAME II

LOYAL TO THE GAME III

By **TJ & Jelissa**

BLOODY COMMAS I & II

SKI MASK CARTEL

By **T.J. Edwards**

IF LOVING HIM IS WRONG...I & II

By **Jelissa**

WHEN THE STREETS CLAP BACK

By **Jibril Williams**

A DISTINGUISHED THUG STOLE MY HEART I & II

By **Meesha**

PUSH IT TO THE LIMIT

By **Bre' Hayes**

BLOOD OF A BOSS **I, II, III & IV**

By **Askari**

THE STREETS BLEED MURDER **I, II & III**

THE HEART OF A GANGSTA I & II

By **Jerry Jackson**

CUM FOR ME

CUM FOR ME 2

CUM FOR ME 3

An **LDP Erotica Collaboration**

BRIDE OF A HUSTLA **I & II**

THE FETTI GIRLS **I, II& III**

By **Destiny Skai**

WHEN A GOOD GIRL GOES BAD

198

The Bossman's Daughters 3
By **Adrienne**

A GANGSTER'S REVENGE **I II III & IV**

THE BOSS MAN'S DAUGHTERS

THE BOSS MAN'S DAUGHTERS II

THE BOSSMAN'S DAUGHTERS III

A SAVAGE LOVE **I & II**

BAE BELONGS TO ME

A HUSTLER'S DECEIT I, II

By **Aryanna**

A KINGPIN'S AMBITON

A KINGPIN'S AMBITION **II**

I MURDER FOR THE DOUGH

By **Ambitious**

TRUE SAVAGE

TRUE SAVAGE II

TRUE SAVAGE **III**

By **Chris Green**

A DOPEBOY'S PRAYER

By **Eddie "Wolf" Lee**

WHAT ABOUT US **I & II**

NEVER LOVE AGAIN

THUG ADDICTION

By **Kim Kaye**

THE KING CARTEL **I, II & III**

By **Frank Gresham**

THESE NIGGAS AIN'T LOYAL **I, II & III**

By **Nikki Tee**

Aryanna
GANGSTA SHYT **I II &III**

By **CATO**

THE ULTIMATE BETRAYAL

By **Phoenix**

BOSS'N UP **I , II & III**

By **Royal Nicole**

I LOVE YOU TO DEATH

By Destiny J

I RIDE FOR MY HITTA

I STILL RIDE FOR MY HITTA

By **Misty Holt**

LOVE & CHASIN' PAPER

By **Qay Crockett**

TO DIE IN VAIN

By **ASAD**

BROOKLYN HUSTLAZ

By **Boogsy Morina**

BROOKLYN ON LOCK I & II

By **Sonovia**

GANGSTA CITY

By **Teddy Duke**

BOOKS BY LDP'S CEO, CA$H

(CLICK TO PURCHASE)

TRUST IN NO MAN

TRUST IN NO MAN 2

TRUST IN NO MAN 3

BONDED BY BLOOD

SHORTY GOT A THUG

THUGS CRY

THUGS CRY 2

THUGS CRY 3

TRUST NO BITCH

TRUST NO BITCH 2

TRUST NO BITCH 3

TIL MY CASKET DROPS

RESTRAINING ORDER

RESTRAINING ORDER 2

IN LOVE WITH A CONVICT

Coming Soon

BONDED BY BLOOD 2

BOW DOWN TO MY GANGSTA

Aryanna

CPSIA information can be obtained
at www.ICGtesting.com
Printed in the USA
LVHW082234011222
734449LV00038B/1674